Allyn's heart was pounding so hard she thought she would faint. "Not one word!" she whispered to Mitchell. "Don't even breathe!"

Mitchell nodded with tears in his eyes. He looked petrified.

Just then, she saw one of the men! He was walking into the alleyway! She took Mitchell's hand and squeezed it. There were loud steps — closer and closer …

Allyn's
Embarrassing
&
Mysterious
Irish Adventures

Carol McGinley

Illustrated by Linda Lefevre Murray

P.O. Box 513
Apex, NC 27502

Cover Design: Pam Varney, Piedmont Litho
Production: Jan Cheves

All photos used by permission.
Cover Photos: "Girl — a Guide at Bantry House" (Bantry, Ireland) by Rénata
Holzbachova and Philippe Bénet; the Cliffs of Moher and Bunratty Castle
provided courtesy of the Irish Tourist Board.
Additional Photos: "Girl — a Guide at Bantry House" in chapter headings by
Rénata Holzbachova and Philippe Bénet; "Irish Bed-and-Breakfast" and
"Sheep in Northern Ireland" color photo by Carol McGinley; all other photos
courtesy of the Irish Tourist Board.

First Printing: January 1999

ISBN: 1-892671-00-X

Books are available at quantity discounts. For ordering information, contact:
AGA Publishing, PO Box 513, Apex, NC 27502. Phone: (919) 387-4568.
Fax (919) 303-7111. Major credit cards accepted.

Library of Congress Catalog Card Number: 98-73200

Publisher's Cataloging-in-Publication
(Provided by Quality Books, Inc.)

McGinley, Carol.
    Allyn's embarrassing & mysterious Irish adventures /
Carol McGinley ; illustrated by Linda Lefevre Murray. --
1st ed.
    p. cm.
    ISBN: 1-892671-00-X
    SUMMARY: A twelve-year-old American girl and her
little brother travel to Ireland with their mother, and
things get tense when the children overhear drug
smuggling plans.

    1. Ireland--Social life and customs--20th century--
Juvenile fiction. 2. Drug traffic--Ireland--Juvenile
fiction. I. Title II. Title: Allyn's embarrassing and
mysterious Irish adventures

PZ7.M16772A1 1999   [Fic]
                              QBI98-972

Printed in the United States of America

To

Stacey, Michael,
Matthew & Christie

And in memory of
Catherine E. Carberry,
who wanted to see Ireland

Contents

Big News

Allyn stumbled out of bed, looked at herself in the vanity mirror, grabbed a pillow, and screamed into it. Her freckles were alive! They were reproducing! It wasn't easy to be twelve. It wasn't easy to resemble an Irish setter.

Allyn plopped back down on the bed and daydreamed that gorgeous Jeremy Sherwin was swinging on vines across town and heading for *her* windowsill.

"Jeremy," she whispered, "you don't know I'm alive, but I kiss the front of your locker at least twenty times a day."

"Allyn! Allyn! Are you up?" called her mother. "Honey, you'll be late if you haven't gotten your shower yet!"

1

"Don't worry, Mom! I'll be ready!"

Allyn threw her pajamas on the bed, plunged into the shower water, and whistled a lovesong, with Jeremy in mind. In a few minutes, she was attacking the long, tomato-red hair with a blowdryer. Maybe one day she would stop tying her hair back, let her bangs grow "naturally," and audition for the monster spot in a horror film.

"Breakfast is ready, Allyn! You need to hurry!"

"Okay, Mom! I'm coming!"

Opening her wardrobe, Allyn stared at the pathetic choices. If only she were a child star! Child stars had splashy dresses, wild shoes and designer underwear! Instead, Allyn had out-of-date, tasteless things she had bought when still a "kid" in the sixth grade. But now ... now she needed thrilling clothes with style and romantic appeal! She'd have to look in the *Spiegel Catalog* under "Candlelight Dinner Apparel."

When she had dressed and run downstairs, Mitchell greeted her with a groan and said, "Finally."

Mitchell the Pain was nine. Allyn was sure the hospital had goofed and exchanged a human, intelligent baby for Mitchell. Someday Mitchell's real parents would leave their jungle nest, swoop by, and carry Mitchell back where he would fit right in — some place where he'd wear the same dirty pants for years and never brush his teeth.

"You don't understand women, Mitchell. You don't understand our complex needs," Allyn said smugly and stuffed her mouth with pancake.

"She's nuts, Mom."

Mitchell's teeth were purple, and Mrs. Gallagher rushed him off to the bathroom to brush them.

Ten minutes later, Allyn was on the bus and heading for Benson Junior High. Even this early, sunlight was baking the bus. It was September 16, but Allyn lived in North Carolina, far enough south for summer heat to stretch through the end of September. For Southerners, summer meant five months of shorts and "warfare deodorant." Allyn was sure it was the same stuff they used in fire extinguishers.

It wasn't easy to be a seventh-grader. You were lowly scum in the eyes of upperclassmen. At least Allyn's best friend Sally was going to Benson, too.

As the bus neared the school, Sally held out her nails to catch the sun. "Isn't this polish great, Al? It's 'Tenderly Twilight Tango-Mango' — made by Dream Cosmetics. You know the ad: 'Products for the discerning woman who lives for those special moments.'"

Allyn nodded in admiration. "It sure says 'discerning woman' to me, Sal." Opening a compact, Allyn stared at her eyebrows and then covered them with her hand. "I wish my mom would let me pluck these or use weedkiller or something." Allyn stood up and waited for the line to leave the bus. "Hey, Sal, did you know that Jeremy's got gym second period, too?"

"Yeah, I knew 'cause Jennifer Whiting's got his whole schedule written on her notebook," Sally answered, holding out a lemon drop for Allyn.

"No, thanks. Jen Whiting? She doesn't really *know* him, does she?"

"No! Are you kidding? No, she's just been tracking him. When Jen wants information, she's a tabloid tailing a movie star."

"It's hopeless for Jen, and it's hopeless for me," Allyn told her, hurrying through the back door and up the stairs to the lockers. "He won't notice an ugly seventh-grader when every girl in the ninth grade thinks he's great."

Sally hurried to keep up. "Al! Come on, Al, you're pretty! You're not ugly at all!"

Allyn turned toward her with a look of intense gravity. "Maybe not *upchuck-your-lunch* ugly, but face it, Sal, I'd get something like Miss Congeniality or Miss Good Sport in a beauty pageant."

They continued down the crowded hall, and it was tough to keep a conversation going. "Did you study for science?" Allyn yelled above the noise.

Grabbing the back of Allyn's shirt, Sally pulled her to the side of the crowd. "Wow, it gets worse every day! I hope nobody smashes my hands," said Sally, looking at the expensive gleam of Tango-

Mango. "Science? No, I figure, why try to convince people that I'm smart? I'll be in fashion design, Al. I don't need brains for that. I need *creativity!*"

The warning bell rang, and from that point on, the day went downhill. Mr. Greer's science test was a killer. He warned the class that their answers had better make sense: "Don't you dare tell me about your mother's violets when I ask you to explain the Greenhouse Effect!"

By the time Allyn had climbed off the bus and headed home, she felt like a boot camp survivor. *Fiona*, she thought. *I'll cheer myself up with hot fudge on the new frozen yogurt, and I'll re-read my Ireland letter.*

Allyn ran upstairs to get her letter from Fiona, made her sundae, and sat at the kitchen table. For two years, Fiona O'Cleary had been her penpal. In catechism class, the priest had passed out the names and addresses of international kids wanting to write to Americans. Fiona lived in Glengariff, on the southern tip of Ireland. It was deep in a valley, near a place called Bantry Bay. Fiona had written that all kinds of tropical flowers grew there because of the sheltering effect of the mountains. Her town was unusual, because most of Ireland was chilly all through the year.

Fiona's last letter was different, though — sadder. Fiona was talking about problems in her family and in Ireland in general. It surprised Allyn that many

Irish teenagers would have to leave Ireland just to get good jobs.

The problem that worried Fiona most, however, was that someone was selling illegal drugs in Glengariff, and she was afraid her older sister was buying them. The idea of drugs was not unusual to Allyn, because many of the public schools in America had drug problems. She knew that even at Benson there were kids that sold drugs. Just over the last year, both Allyn's mother and father had, separately, talked to her about the danger of taking a drug.

Allyn's father lived in Raleigh, the state capital; his house was about twenty-five minutes away. He and Allyn's mother had divorced a few years ago, and now Allyn and Mitchell saw him on weekends and holidays. It always hurt to watch him drive away, back to his own home. Slowly, though, Allyn was noticing that the divorce was starting to feel a little more "normal."

"I'm home!" came a voice from the hall.

"Hi, Mom!" yelled Mitchell from the family room.

"I'm in the kitchen, Mom," Allyn told her. "How was work?"

"Not bad today, Allie. I finally have a replacement, and Dr. Mueller approved it."

"Replacement? He didn't fire you, did he?"

"Not exactly," said Mrs. Gallagher, putting groceries away as though nothing unusual had happened.

"'Not exactly'? 'Not exactly'! What does that mean?" Allyn got up from the table, leaned on the counter, and stared at her mother intensely. "Are they suspending you for bad behavior or something?"

Her mother started to laugh.

"Really — you can be honest with me, Mom. Did you get some bills mixed up? Did you sock some poor old lady with a bill for six hundred bucks — just to clean her dentures?"

Her mother shook her head from side to side. Mrs. Gallagher was too full of laughter to talk.

Allyn thought her mother was remarkably calm about getting "replaced" at work. Her mother loved working for Dr. Mueller; the hours were right, the office was close, and the people were friendly.

"Allie, I needed someone to replace me while I'm on vacation," said Mrs. Gallagher with a strange expression.

"On vacation? You mean like Christmas?"

"Well, more like October."

"October?" Allyn was thoroughly confused. "Where are you going in October?"

"Actually, you should ask me where *we* are going in October."

"We? Who's we?"

"All of us — you, me, Mitchell, and even your Aunt Georgette."

Allyn ran to the refrigerator and shook her mother's arm. "Confess! Confess, Mom! What have you been keeping from me?"

"I had my reasons, Allie," answered Mrs. Gallagher with a warm smile. "In just a few weeks, your Aunt Georgette is flying all of us to — "

"Los Angeles! Movie capital of the world!" interrupted Allyn.

"Well ... maybe another time. No, this time we're not going west — nowhere near California." Mrs. Gallagher hesitated, trying to build up as much suspense as possible.

"Cut to the chase, Mom!"

"Ireland!" she answered with a huge smile. "The dining room, Allie, in ten minutes! Be there!" Mrs. Gallagher rushed out of the room and up the stairs.

The Itinerary

Allyn jumped toward the ceiling and shouted, "Yes! Yes! It's incredibly perfect!"

"Allie, *please*," said her mother. "Let's keep the glasses from shattering."

Mrs. Gallagher's arms were full of maps and booklets, and she spread these on the dining room table.

Mitchell stared at the maps sadly. "Couldn't we go to Walt Disney World? Please, Mom."

"Maybe next year, Mitchell. But I guarantee you're going to like Ireland."

Three years older than Mitchell, Allyn understood what a big deal it was to go to Europe. She put her hands on her hips and started circling the table. "Ireland. Fiona's Ireland. We're really going. This

9

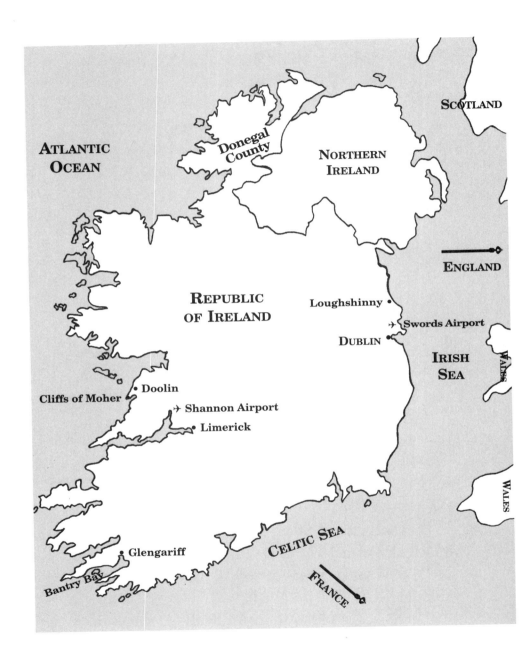

isn't a dream. I'm not hallucinating. In three weeks, we'll be going to — "

"You're makin' me dizzy, Al!" complained Mitchell.

"Look at this, Allie. Let me show you where we're going." Her mother pointed to an airplane on the map. "We'll fly in here, to Shannon Airport. And then we're going west, all the way to the ocean. You'll love the Cliffs of Moher. And then north to Donegal County. Both the Gallaghers and my great grandparents, the Connollys, are from there, so you and Mitchell should feel right at home."

"Are we gonna get indoor pools?" asked Mitchell, looking at a booklet of Bunratty Castle.

"Uh, no — but we'll stay in B-and-B's," answered his mother, "and you'll get to see how Irish people live."

"Are B-and-B's like inflatable tents or something?"

"Mitchell!" interrupted Allyn. "Don't you know anything about other countries? B-and-B's are barns and bunkhouses!"

Laughing, Mrs. Gallagher managed to reply, "That's not exactly it, Allie. 'B-and-B' stands for 'Bed-and-Breakfast.' It means that Irish families open up their homes and give tourists both a bedroom and a good breakfast in the morning."

"Won't they see us in our underwear?" asked Mitchell, looking at his mother as though she were making a big mistake.

An Irish Bed-and-Breakfast

Mrs. Gallagher shook her head. "No — no, Mitchell. Usually these homes have separate areas for guests. You and Allie will have a room, and I'll have one with your Aunt Georgette. We might have to walk down a hall to the bathroom, but we're all bringing robes. I promise you solemnly, Mitchell — they won't see us in our underwear."

"Mom, wouldn't it be weird to have people stay with us like that, around all the time?" asked Allyn. "I wouldn't like it."

"They do it because they have to, Allie — for the money. In general, the Irish don't have as much money as Americans do."

Allyn remembered what her penpal Fiona had said about the Irish summers. "Won't it be freezing in October, Mom? Fiona says it's cool in Ireland, even in July."

"It will be a little colder. We'll take jackets and warm sweaters."

"Will it be cold enough to snow in Ireland?" Mitchell asked in a hopeful voice.

"Oh, sorry again, Mitchell. It won't be that cold. I don't think they get much snow there, anyway," Mrs. Gallagher told him.

Mitchell slapped his hand on top of one of the booklets. "No rides, no indoor pools, no snow! What makes Ireland so great, anyway?"

"Mitchell!" Allyn was disgusted. "Don't you realize how *far* we're going? We'll fly over the WHOLE

ATLANTIC OCEAN! We'll probably see huge battleships from the U.S. Navy — right from our plane
window!"

Mitchell folded his arms and accepted this new
information with a puzzled look. "Is that true,
Mom?"

"Here, let's look at the map, Mitchell. Here's
New York City. We'll leave here, and fly over all this
water, and land here — at Shannon. It will take us
about seven hours."

"What about the battleships?" he asked, keeping
his arms folded and trying his best to look tough.

"We'll be flying pretty high, Mitchell. But you
might see some ships in New York," answered his
mother, pulling out a map of Northern Ireland.

Mitchell didn't say anything, but looked satisfied with this answer.

Allyn leaned over the map of Northern Ireland.
"Mom, this is a separate country from the rest of
Ireland."

Mrs. Gallagher smiled. "Yes, Allie."

"But we aren't going *there*, are we?"

"When we leave Donegal, we'll drive through
this little corner of Northern Ireland. It's the fastest
way to Dublin," answered her mother.

"But, Mom, even though they're supposed to
have peace, there was fighting there for lots and lots
of years! We might get blown up!"

Mitchell jumped up from his chair and shouted,
"Great! Great! Danger! We're gonna face danger!"

Mrs. Gallagher grabbed her head as though she suddenly felt ill.

Allyn looked at her and laughed. "It's okay, Mom. Mitchell and I would much rather face Northern Ireland than a day at school. Anything's safer than gym class."

"Allie, Mitchell, hear this." Mrs. Gallagher was speaking slowly and calmly. "My sister — your reliable Aunt Georgette — said that even during the worst fighting, parts of Northern Ireland were safe for tourists. Although there have been terrible casualties in Belfast and some other spots, the media made it sound as though the country was one big war zone. I know this will disappoint you, Mitchell, but danger isn't in the itinerary!"

"So what's an itin—thing?" Mitchell asked, with his legs up on the chair and his knees tight against the edge of the table.

"It's our plan for the vacation, Mitchell — what we're going to see and when." Mrs. Gallagher started searching through a pile of papers for something.

"Don't you know anything, Mitchell?" Allyn felt particularly impatient with her brother today. "An itinerberry! Everybody needs an itinerberry when they go into a dangerous country!"

"Allyn!" Mrs. Gallagher's face was getting red. "Please — *please* get the idea of danger out of your head! We're driving through just a small part of Northern Ireland. Though the landscape is supposed to be beautiful, we're just driving through. Okay?"

"Okay. So how long will the whole trip take?" Allyn was hoping she'd miss at least three tests and maybe an oral report.

"We'll be gone two weeks."

"Two weeks! Yea!" Mitchell was excited again. "Maybe they'll kick us out of school, and you'll have to get Chester McKoy to tutor me. He could get me through all the fourth grade stuff, Mom! He used to be a teacher, and I bet he'd even do it for free. Can you tell the principal it's okay if he expels me?"

"No, Mitchell, I sure won't," answered Mrs. Gallagher, looking at a sheet with the words 'Ireland Itinerary' at the top. "I've already called your teacher, and I've called three of your teachers, too, Allie. You'll both have assignments to do on the trip, so we'll have to set aside some time for homework."

"Darn," said Allyn.

"Darn," Mitchell echoed. "But what if we can't get back, Mom? What if there's something wrong with the plane, and we have to stay in Ireland for months? Then can I get expelled?"

Mrs. Gallagher laughed. "Honey, I wouldn't count on that happening." Mrs. Gallagher put a map of the eastern part of Ireland near Mitchell. "See this airplane on the map?"

Mitchell nodded.

"This is where we'll turn in our rental car, and we'll get a plane back. It's Swords."

"Swords? Do they have sword fights and stuff there? Do we get to keep one? Oh, please, Mom!" Mitchell pleaded. "I wanna bring back a sword — a real one!"

Mrs. Gallagher put her hands on her temples again. "Swords *Airport*. It's only the name. No sword fights, no danger, no months of waiting for a plane. But if I make through this vacation, it'll be a miracle."

"Mom's had enough, Mitch," said Allyn in her supervisor voice. "Let's be adults. We've got three weeks to ask her about swords and bombs and packing tips." Allyn waved her arm dramatically. "Come, Mitchell! Let Mom deal with her nervous breakdown in peace!"

As Allyn led Mitchell away, she glanced behind her. Her mother's head was bent way down over the table, and her body shook with the strong bursts of her muffled laughter.

Spider in the Dark

Allyn thought there couldn't possibly be any better surprise than finding out she was flying to Ireland for two weeks. On the bus ride to school, she told Sally, and Sally screamed as though bats were camping in her underwear. All through the day at school, Allyn couldn't concentrate on anything but being in a foreign country. Her Aunt Georgette had a wild side, and Allyn knew the trip to Ireland would be a crazy adventure.

Finally, after a day of daydreaming, she got off the bus and walked to the mailbox out of habit. She flipped through the pile of mail and almost didn't notice her name on one of the envelopes.

"It's from Dad," she mumbled to herself.

Allyn opened the envelope and read as she

walked down the long driveway. It was windy, and her long red hair was blowing so much she could hardly read. She dropped her bookbag, sat in the middle of the driveway, held one side of her hair back, and read with her mouth open. She couldn't move! She could hardly breathe! Carefully, very carefully, she read the lines again, just to make sure she wasn't dreaming. Every sentence made her heart beat faster. *Tickets — Darryl James — Loughshinny, Ireland — October 20 — in person.* Darryl James! Darryl James was her favorite singer in the entire world! *He* would be in Loughshinny, Ireland, when *she* would be in Loughshinny, and her father had arranged something unbelievable.

The tears were coming too fast for Allyn to read the letter again. She cried because she was too packed with happiness to do anything else. One by one, the facts organized themselves in her mind: the concert would be in Loughshinny; American television cameras would be filming the concert; her father had contacted someone who knew Darryl James's manager and had bought four front-row tickets for Allyn, Mitchell, her mother, and her Aunt George for the concert.

Allyn wiped her eyes, picked up her bookbag, and sprinted to the door. She dropped her bag in the front hall and danced like a ballerina through every room on the first floor. "It's marvelous!" she shouted. "It's magnificent!"

Mitchell got home a few minutes later, and Allyn was still dancing and announcing the news to the world. "It's a dream! It's stupendous! It's — "

"You're givin' me a headache!" Mitchell told her, as he ran up the stairs and made a barricade with his army equipment.

Mitchell did not appreciate ballet, Allyn decided. She plopped on the floor of the family room and called Sally, who loved Darryl James passionately. Allyn had to keep the receiver away from her ear because Sally's reaction sounded like something from a jungle movie. When Allyn tried to calm her down, Sally called herself "a woman temporarily lost to this world."

Sally insisted that Allyn *had* to take her to Ireland, too. "I'll do anything!" pleaded Sally. "I'll squeeze into a kennel box! I'll sell my assets!"

"You don't have any assets, Sal," Allyn reminded her. "You just get an allowance."

"I've got my great-grandmother's hope chest."

"Sally, that's for your marriage. I think it's like a dowry or a bribe or something."

"Marriage is a small price to pay," replied Sally in despair.

"I'll get his autograph for you," promised Allyn. "I'll tell him to put 'Sally darling' on it."

This had a good effect. Sally sounded better, and for the next two weeks she talked to Allyn about all the possible ways Darryl James could say "I love you" on paper.

By the time her flight to Ireland was just one week away, Allyn was so tired of the autograph idea that she thought it would be easier just to hide Sally in a duffelbag and to take her along. Aunt George, however, had told Allyn to "pack as light as feathers," and Sally's fingernails alone weighed more than that.

Sally's real name was "Selina Leigh." Allyn had called her "Sally" for six years, and it usually fit. There were times, though, when Sally's behavior was just as strange and exotic as a *Selina*, and Allyn decided that she should call her Selina during those out-of-this-world episodes.

While Allyn was lying in her room and looking at pictures of Irish cliffs, her mother reminded her to get ready. It was Friday night — the night when all good Catholics went to confession. Confession, as Allyn had explained it to her Baptist friend Julie, was a time when you told the priest that you had hurt other people and hadn't done the things that you should have. Then the priest said that God loved and forgave you, and you knelt again and prayed something short and stared at the statues that stared back. Then you left, feeling like Ajax had scrubbed up your soul.

"Please, Mom! Please!" Mitchell was pleading desperately. "I'll drop over! I will! If I try to walk, I'm a goner!"

This kind of protest was familiar. Every time it was confession night, Mitchell was sure Death was around the corner. He hated going to confession, and he always had mysterious symptoms. Tonight there were awful pains in both earlobes, a numb spot on his leg, and yellow stuff growing out of his gums (he had just eaten cheesy chips).

His mother was unmoved. "You're going, Mitchell. We'll bury you in the churchyard in your tennis shoes. Allie, get the shovel."

On the way to the church, Mitchell was as somber as a man viewing his own casket. He had to be shoved through the door of the sanctuary and into the back pew. There they all waited for one of the confessional "closets" to be unoccupied. There were two confessionals at the back of the sanctuary, and a little light above the door went off whenever someone left the confessional. The priest sat in a barely-lit section between the two "closets," and he opened a little panel to his left or right to hear one person at a time. In each of the confessional closets there was a kneeler that faced the middle section, but it was tar-dark in there until the priest opened his little panel. Then there was just enough light to see your own nose. Unfortunately, Mitchell was afraid of the dark, and that's why he dreaded confession.

Mrs. Gallagher went into one confessional, and Allyn waited for her turn. In less than a minute, the light went off over the other confessional, and Allyn went in and knelt. Her mother's confession time had just begun, so Allyn found herself kneeling and waiting for what felt like a long time — long enough to imagine that she felt something creeping over her arm. The word "spider" shot across her mind like a firecracker! Allyn sped out of the confessional, gasped for breath, and dropped into the pew beside Mitchell.

"Mitchell! A spider attacked me!" she whispered with a white face. "Right there in the confessional — a Catholic spider jumped on my arm!"

"You sure, Al?" Mitchell asked. "Did you see it? Was it a black widow?"

"I didn't see anything, but I'm sure it was a spider, Mitch. I think it was one of those big hairy ones — with pointed teeth!" Allyn told him.

She was glad that the church was almost completely empty. One man had just left, and there was one old woman sitting in the first row of the church. Allyn was sure she was almost deaf, because she never turned around to frown or to tell them they were being too loud.

"Know what, Al? I'm gonna go in," Mitchell said in his commando voice. "If there's a tarantula or something in there, I gotta protect people by gettin' rid of it."

"Mitchell, are you crazy? It's the confessional! The confessional! You hate the place! And worse — we're talking about a killer insect! We're talking about poisonous bites and slow, agonizing death!"

"I know, Al, but I brought my military stuff with me, and I'm gonna be okay."

Allyn shook her head in disbelief. "Wow, Mitch. You are really changing. I can't believe you're going to go in there." Allyn couldn't hide the admiration.

"I'm gettin' ready for the real army, Al. I gotta be tough," said Mitchell proudly, and he walked to the back.

Allyn had watched Mitchell take something out of his pocket, but she couldn't tell what it was. She watched the confessional carefully and expected him to dart out any moment.

Finally, Allyn's mother emerged from the other confessional, and she was halfway to the pew when Mitchell burst out of the other door and yelled, "Fire! Fire! We need water quick!"

Seconds later, the priest ran out of his cubicle and raced toward the rectory. Allyn was in shock. Smoke was coming from Mitchell's section, and Mitchell was filling his shoes with holy water and throwing it into the confessional. Mrs. Gallagher screamed and pulled Mitchell away because the smoke was getting thick, and Allyn saw the old woman shuffle as fast as she could go out of the church!

It all happened so fast! The priest had come back with a fire extinguisher and two other priests, and in a minute there was no more fire.

Father Dawes was understanding but firm, and he took Mitchell aside to get the facts. Mitchell had been looking for huge hairy spiders with a small candle (brought from home) and a match. When Father Dawes snapped open the panel, Mitchell was so shocked that he dropped the candle onto the kneeler material, and it smoked up the closet like a wiener roast.

Mitchell explained that he was afraid of the dark, and Father Dawes explained how quickly smoke can kill people. Then Mitchell apologized and asked God to forgive him for the burnt offering in His closet; and Father Dawes assured Mitchell that even Catholic spiders wouldn't be allowed in the confessionals.

Things were getting resolved when Allyn heard sirens in the distance. "There must be a fire nearby, Mom," she said, and both of them looked at each other with the same awful thought. A firetruck sped to a halt in front of the church, and two firemen appeared in the sanctuary to ask what section was burning. The old woman had scuffed to a phone and told firemen that the church was a flaming shish-kabob.

It was very embarrassing! Allyn was sure she would see her name in the morning paper:

Allyn Gallagher's Brother Torches Sacred Confessional!

God is pressing charges: "Our Lord will make a rare appearance in court," says priest.

Everyone gave Mitchell a fire lecture, and Allyn was glad that no one took a snapshot of them for the F.B.I. On the way home, Allyn was daydreaming about Jeremy Sherwin hopping a plane for Ireland, and then she remembered something. "Mom! I never actually got to confess! Shouldn't we go back?"

In the front seat, Mrs. Gallagher had been giving Mitchell a lecture, and slowly, the two turned around and glared at her ... without one word.

The Pizza Fiasco

It was a good night to go out for dinner. In just two days they would be in Ireland, and Allyn was too excited to be satisfied with anything routine. Just last week, Sally had told her about Pizza World, the place where Mrs. Gallagher was taking them for dinner. Mitchell had pleaded with his mother to do something different, so they decided to go get pizza.

Sally's expert restaurant review of Pizza World was that the food was great but that it was "the kind of joint where people go when they have no cultural taste." It was a typical Selina Leigh comment.

At six o'clock, Allyn, Mitchell, and Mrs. Gallagher slid into a crust-colored booth, curved at the end of a strange triangle-like table. The table was painted like a slice of pizza, and the whole effect made Allyn want anything but a pizza pie.

After the waitress took their order, Allyn told her mother, "Boy, this place gets a tacky award."

Mrs. Gallagher laughed. "I know, but look at all these people. The food must be good."

"Don't knock it, Al!" said Mitchell, using his finger to trace the outline of a huge piece of painted sausage. "Ben Ridder said it's got the best pizza in Cary. And he should know — his family goes out to eat all the time."

Just then the background music changed, and Allyn thought it sounded like the "Battle Hymn of the Republic."

A little child in the place cried out, "Look, Mommy!"

Allyn turned in the booth, and there it was: a procession of human pizza toppings dancing down the hallway from the kitchen. A huge olive, mushroom, pepperoni, cheese slice, onion, and a green pepper danced and sang the daily specials to the tune of the "Battle Hymn of the Republic":

"We're mozzarella, peppers, onions, pepperoni, too!
We're the toppings on the pizza made especially for you!
Try 'Deluxe': you'll get all six of us for just a buck or two
At Pizza World today!"

Allyn thought that was bad enough, but then they sang the chorus:

"Try the specials on the black—board!
Salads, coffee free, as fea—tured;
Garlic bread comes, too, if or—dered
At Pizza World today!"

Allyn looked at Mitchell, and he was mesmerized. She leaned toward her mother and whispered, "It must be a sacrilege to do that to the 'Battle Hymn of the Republic.'" Now that she was twelve, she was noticing all the weird things that people did for money: dressing up as a green pepper, for instance. Fortunately, the "specials song" lasted just a minute or two.

"Mom, have you told Aunt George about the Darryl James concert? She'll love it! I know she's got one of his albums."

"I finally called her late Sunday night, Allie, and she's going to write to your father to thank him. She *is* excited! And she's glad we've got all our reservations and trip details worked out. It takes an incredible amount of planning to go out of the country for two weeks. Honestly, though, if she hadn't already been in Ireland, I wouldn't have a clue how to plan for this thing."

"She went with Uncle Todd last time, didn't she?"

"Yeah. I hope the trip won't bring up all that pain again," answered Mrs. Gallagher, as the waitress arrived with the food.

"Mom, she knew he was dying even before she decided to marry him, didn't she?"

"Uh-huh. It was a brave thing to do, Allie. She loved him, and that's all that mattered to her."

"Mom, let's do lots of fun stuff to cheer her up there!" suggested Mitchell. "Let's catch bait and fish and camp out and pet the sheep."

Mrs. Gallagher laughed, but Allyn wasn't amused.

"Mitchell," Allyn told him, "to Aunt George, catching live bait isn't exactly the thrill of a lifetime, get it? We need to be sensitive to what *she* likes — to do something that she'll never forget for the rest of her life. Like, maybe we can get in the autograph line, and then, at just the right moment, push her hard at Darryl James so he catches her in a passionate, romantic embrace."

Mrs. Gallagher choked on her garlic bread.

Allyn patted her mother's back. "Are you okay, Mom?"

Mrs. Gallagher nodded and took a drink, as battle music grew in the background.

"Mom, I gotta do a big nose blow," announced Mitchell. "So can I do it in the bathroom?"

Allyn rolled her eyes.

"Okay, Mitchell," answered Mrs. Gallagher, "but

come right back, and don't stop to talk to anybody. It's right down that hall toward the back."

In a flash, Mitchell was out of the booth and gone.

The "toppings," in the meantime, were continuing their little pizza chorus, and Allyn tried to ignore it. She talked to her mother about her Uncle Todd's smoking and why people don't understand that smoking can kill them. Then, out of the corner of her eye, Allyn noticed Mitchell running back toward the table.

As Mitchell tried to dart around Mr. Onion, who was doing his little "circle dance," Mr. Onion took a step back and Mitchell plowed into him! The force sent Mr. Onion stumbling across the circle and right into Mr. Pepperoni, who was so top-heavy that he crashed into the salad bar! Carrots and dressings and sliced eggs exploded out of the bar and hit the booths and customers behind it!

Then Mr. Onion tried to help Mr. Pepperoni up, but Mr. Pepperoni was so upset that he picked up what was left of the cottage cheese and threw it at Mr. Onion. Mr. Onion was quick enough to duck, but it hit Ms. Mushroom in the face!

At that point, Allyn ran out of the booth to retrieve Mitchell, who was sitting on the floor in shock. When she got near him, though, she slipped on some spilled peach halves and knocked down Ms. Mushroom, who couldn't see very well through the

cottage cheese. Ms. Mushroom was absolutely furious. She yelled at Mr. Mozzarella, as though he had pushed her down. Then she picked up someone's pizza and threw it at Mr. Mozzarella, who was so surprised that he stumbled backward and fell into some man's lap. The man was upset. He shoved Mr. Mozzarella across the room — toward Mr. Pepperoni, who had finally managed to stand again.

By the time Mrs. Gallagher reached Allyn and Mitchell, pizzas were flying everywhere. "It's getting dangerous!" yelled Mrs. Gallagher. She pulled both of them into the back hall of the restaurant and told them not to move an inch. She had pizza all over her new beige sweater, and her face was beyond words.

Allyn looked at the main room in disbelief. Pizza World was a disaster area! And who was responsible for it all? Who had sprinted back from the bathroom with no thought for the safety of mankind? Allyn Lane Gallagher knew! It was Mitchell! "Mitchell," she whispered in a forbidding tone, "they'll get you for this! You're Public Enemy Number One!"

Mitchell looked at her like those shocked foxes when they realize they're in an English hunt.

The police had arrived, but no one paid any attention to Mrs. Gallagher's apologies. Allyn and Mitchell could hear the police questioning the manager, and then they heard their mother trying to get herself made liable for the whole nasty mess. Sometimes Allyn wished her mother were a little less honest!

Allyn was sure it was a miracle when no one cared that Mitchell caused the ruin of Pizza World. Instead, the senior manager just kept scowling at the toppings and repeating something about "behavior unbecoming to professional entertainers."

Allyn was a little disappointed that Mitchell wasn't booked. He was, after all, a public nuisance.

"If you ever run in a restaurant again, Mitchell, you'll stay in your room until you're old enough for wrinkles." It was the only thing Mrs. Gallagher said the entire way home.

Mitchell slid down so far in the seat that he blended into the vinyl. Allyn looked at him and then at all the different foods smashed on her jeans and shirt. She thought it was a good thing they were leaving for Ireland in two days. Mitchell was turning America into a dangerous place.

Marley's Ghost
Flies Aer Lingus

When Allyn woke on Saturday, there was rain splattering the window, but nothing could discourage her. This was October 7 — the day on her plane tickets, the day she would leap over the Atlantic Ocean in a luxury jet!

Allyn had packed and re-packed. Her mother had given her a list of essential things, but she still had room for a few extras, like her binoculars. Allyn wondered what weird "extras" Mitchell had stuffed into *his* suitcase. Allyn was glad her mother had packed the essentials for Mitchell, because he always forgot crucial things like a change of underwear and a toothbrush. On vacations with her father, sometimes Mitchell's mouth looked like seaweed.

"Aunt George!" shouted Mitchell. "Aunt George is here! I'll get Paul!"

By the time Allyn reached the door, Mitchell was halfway down the street and headed toward Paul Daniel's house. Paul was a senior in high school, and today he was driving them to the airport in his old van. Allyn wished her father could drive them, but he was in Chicago on business and wouldn't be back until next week.

Allyn hugged her Aunt George.

"Are you as excited as I am, Allie?"

"More!"

"Right on time, George!" said Mrs. Gallagher as she lugged two heavy suitcases down the stairs.

"Hey, let me help you, Liz!" Aunt George rushed up the steps to grab one of the suitcases.

"Mom, Mitchell's out there without an umbrella. I'll bet he'll have to change again," Allyn told her mother.

"He's a challenge to my sanity, George," said Mrs. Gallagher, checking to make sure all the suitcases had nametags.

"He's an adorable burst of energy, isn't he?" answered Aunt George.

Allyn decided that Aunt George had the gift of seeing a little piece of good in a big batch of trouble.

In a few minutes, Paul was there, and when Mitchell had changed again, they left for the airport. The ride went fast, and in less than an hour they were walking through the hijacker trap — the X-ray machine that told police who was a terrorist or a mobster. Mitchell loved the trap. He wanted to stay there and watch for underworld assassins.

"Mitch, they aren't going to catch anybody here!" Allyn told him with authority. "Spies and hijackers don't live in North Carolina! They live in places like Budapest and Vienna and Brooklyn!"

Mitchell looked disappointed, but he revived when the loudspeaker announced that they could board the plane. All four of them joined a big wave of people moving through a tunnel to the plane's door.

"This is style, Mitch," whispered Allyn. "In crummy airports you have to walk outside to get on, and your hair blows up like Frankenstein's bride."

"I can see the pilot!" Mitchell whispered excitedly. "Look at all the stuff on the panel."

Mitchell loved dials. He had told the family that he wanted to be the first man to leave the solar system.

When Allyn was particularly angry at Mitchell, she thought of new ways to send him out of the solar system. Her favorite idea was to wrap him in a rocket-powered box with a big red bow. She'd write "Whitman's Sampler for Alien Species" on it. It was a delicious thought.

When they were seated, the stewardess held up a card, but no one paid any attention to her. Allyn was amazed that no one seemed to care what they should do if the air went bad or the engines died and they had to emergency-land in somebody's tomato garden. She wondered if people were just too scared to think about it.

"Look, Al! We're gettin' ready to floor it!" Mitchell said, as the engines got louder and louder.

Soon they were tilting upward, and Allyn's back was glued to the seat. It was funny to see high buildings shrink down to goldfish food.

Allyn loved the feeling of gliding on nothing. She closed her eyes, pushed the seat back, and felt very comfortable.

Her arm. Mitchell was shaking and shaking her arm. "What are you doin' that for, Mitch?" She felt strange and groggy.

"New York, Al! It's New York!"

"It can't be New York, Mitch! We just left," said Allyn, having trouble getting her eyes open.

"No, Al. You slept through the orange juice and the pilot talking and everything."

Mitchell was right. Allyn could see a filmy kind of sunshine, and they were very close to the ground. In a few minutes, the plane's strong brakes kept them from falling off the edge of the runway.

New York — city of glamour, city of lights and action! Allyn was sorry that she wouldn't be there long enough to get "discovered." Allyn loved the idea of show business. She just knew that someday a rich producer would notice her goldmine of "hidden potential" and promise her millions to star in his next Broadway play!

It took quite a while to walk all the way to the Irish airline — Aer Lingus — in the terminal. Allyn got a magazine and a hotdog, and she was surprised when Mitchell asked to use the bathroom for the second time in just two hours. He took his carry-bag with him again, too. In fact, he seemed glued to that bag.

When it was time to board, Allyn got more and more excited. This plane was huge! They walked and walked to get to the special business-class section. Aunt George was rich, though not many people knew it, and she had gotten them better seats than coach class. Coach class sounded like royalty to Allyn, and she thought it was strange that on planes it really meant "dirt cheap and uncomfortable."

"This is it, Al," said Mitchell. "Can I have the window first?"

"Okay, Mitch. I can be mature about this. I can be self-sacrificing. But in exactly three-and-a-half hours, I get the window — even if you're asleep, even if you're having the best dream of your life."

"It's a deal." Mitchell strapped in and gingerly put his carry-bag under the seat.

The giant-size plane had two aisles of two seats each along the walls, and in the middle there was a long row of five seats. It was 7:30 in the evening, and they would arrive in Ireland in the middle of the night, at 2:30 a.m. In Ireland, though, the sun would be up, because the time was different there. All the clocks would say it was five hours later — 7:30 a.m. Allyn was sure she would look like morgue material when she got off the plane.

Dinner was supposed to be served around 9:00 p.m., so Allyn and Mitchell played cards for over an hour.

"You look like you're havin' a grand time," said the stewardess, waiting for them to clear the cards off their fold-down trays. "Beef, is it?" she said as she held up a tray of roast beef.

Before Allyn could answer, Mitchell said, "I don't know, Ma'am. It kind of looks like beef to me."

The stewardess laughed, and Allyn understood. "He gets the beef," she told the stewardess. "And I get the chicken."

When the stewardess had moved on, Allyn whispered, "Mitch, that must be the way they talk in Ireland."

Mitchell looked confused and then nudged Allyn to look at a lady across the aisle. She was fifty-fivish; had mile-high teased hair and a mink stole; and she struggled to climb out of the row in the middle of the plane. As the woman got closer, Allyn could see layers of make-up, jewel earrings, and big diamond rings on her fingers.

"I bet that lady has survived three husbands,

Mitchell! I bet she married millionaires and then nagged them into their graves! I bet — " Allyn stopped in mid-thought, remembered she was a shining example of virtue for her brother, and changed the subject. "Hey, Mitch, look at all this styrofoam stuff. What do you think a primitive person, like a cave-dweller, would think of riding on top of clouds and eating hot food out of these tacky containers?"

"I dunno."

"He would do the sensible thing, Mitch. He would leave the food and eat the containers."

No response.

Allyn decided that humor was lost on Mitchell.

"I gotta go to the bathroom. Let me out, Al."

"Again? Are you ill? 'Fess up, Mitchell, do you have a nasty disease you haven't told us about?"

"You're bein' weird. Just let me out."

"Okay, but why don't I just watch your carry-bag for you while you're gone," said Allyn, grasping for the strap.

"No!" yelled Mitchell, and his face was getting red.

Directly in front of them, Mrs. Gallagher turned around in her seat to see what had happened. Allyn was embarrassed, and she got up nonchalantly to let Mitchell out. By the time Mitchell got back, however, she had worked out a plan. She would pick the right moment and find out what vile secret Mitchell was hiding in that bag.

Allyn was tired, so she closed her eyes once more and tried to sleep before the movie started. When she woke, it was close to 10:30 p.m., and Mitchell was drawing pictures of lizards with high teased hair. They looked very peculiar.

"It's time, Mitch," she said with a scratchy voice.

Amazingly, Mitchell didn't complain. He picked up his bag and moved out, and just after Allyn got comfy at the window, the lights blinked off. Movie time! It was an adventure film — something about divers finding a sunken ship and almost drowning.

Allyn put on her earphones and watched the first half of the movie, and then she noticed that Mitchell's head had slumped and that his mouth was slightly open. He had removed his earphones, and his face was stilled in sleep.

Carefully — so very carefully — Allyn lifted the carry-bag from the floor. It was right in front of Mitchell's legs, but Allyn moved it slowly enough so that it never touched Mitchell.

The plane was dark, except for the changing brightness of the movie. When Allyn unzipped the bag, she tilted it toward the screen and held it open as far as it would stretch. Unfortunately, just then there wasn't much light, because the divers were in a dark underwater scene.

If she moved anything, Mitchell would know that she had looked, so Allyn kept the bag open and waited for a brighter scene. After a few minutes, the divers surfaced, and Allyn threw her hand over her mouth! Something blue! Something had climbed out of the bag — ON ITS OWN! A lizard — a lizard was staring at her on top of the bag, and she couldn't move!

It took Allyn a minute to recognize "Marley's Ghost." This was Mitchell's blue lizard, his skink. Mrs. Gallagher had helped Mitchell name him. "Jacob Marley" was a ghost with bluish skin in Charles Dickens's *A Christmas Carol.*

Allyn bravely put out her hand, but Marley was gone! In a flash, he had disappeared! Allyn quietly put the bag on the floor in front of Mitchell and bent way down to see if she could spot a blue flash under the seats.

"Mitchell's gonna murder me. Mitchell's gonna murder me," Allyn mumbled over and over. Her heartbeat felt like a race car engine, and she had to think of a plan. The movie was winding down, and Allyn noticed that a lot of people were sleeping. It was ridiculous to look for a small blue lizard in a dark airplane, she thought. In less than two hours the sky would be lightening, and Allyn would do the brave thing: she would ask the stewardess to announce casually that Marley had disappeared.

Bad idea. Very bad idea, she thought. Never tell passengers there's a blue lizard loose who might be inching his way toward their underwear.

Maybe she should wake up her mother. No —

maybe Aunt George. Aunt George would understand things like hidden reptiles on an unsuspecting plane.

Panic. What if he were smashed accidentally — by a killer cosmetic case or a mammoth running shoe? What if he crawled up the leg of a stewardess and she socked him flat with a breakfast tray? Horrible ideas filled Allyn's mind.

When the movie ended, Mitchell was still asleep, and the plane was as quiet as a mausoleum. Not realizing how tired she was, Allyn thought she would close her eyes for a few minutes until it was light enough to look for Marley.

Soon, however, she was deep in a dream, and dustbusters — millions of dustbusters — were taking over the earth. They were sucking up everything in their paths! Nothing escaped — not trees, houses, lizards. Screaming! The dustbusters were coming, and people were screaming!

It took a few seconds for Allyn to realize that someone *was* screaming! She managed to open her eyes, and Mitchell was waking at the same time.

"What is it, Al? What's goin' on?"

No! Across the aisle ... on top of the teased hairdo ... caught in a tangle of stiff stickiness ... was a splash of blue.

"Marley!" yelled Mitchell. "That's Marley!"

People were eating breakfast, and the woman — who had jumped up like a jackrabbit — was knock-

ing the folding trays up as she rushed out to the other aisle. "Get it off! Get it off!" she screamed.

A distinguished man in a gray suit leapt to her aid, and using his newspaper, he tried to knock the lizard off. As Allyn watched, the mile-high hair and Marley flew off like a missile! Up! Up and across the entire middle section! And then down — SPLAT — on some woman's coffee and danish.

"Mrs. Hairdo" had the face of a blue ghost. With a hand covering her flat natural hair, she raced off toward the lavatory. Two stewards from first-class rushed in, and soon the danish and the wig and Marley were rolling around in a plastic bag.

"That's mine!" yelled Mitchell, grabbing for the bag. "Don't hurt him! Don't hurt him! That's Marley!"

At that point, Allyn's mother gave her breakfast tray to Aunt George, who looked totally confused, and made a dash for Mitchell. "Mitchell! Mitchell! What in the world have you done?"

The rest is a matter of airline history. Mitchell explained; Allyn explained; Mrs. Gallagher, in her own quiet way, was temporarily beyond furious. Mrs. Hairdo; the coffee and pastry lady; and the row of people with breakfast all over their seats got free airline tickets and drycleaning and new seats for what was left of the flight. Marley got a new container and a new home. He would live out his happy lizard life wherever the airline chose to take him.

Mitchell was upset about losing "custody" of Marley, but under the circumstances he knew he was getting off easy. Mrs. Gallagher paid a fine for bringing wildlife on the plane, and Allyn and Mitchell got the lecture of their lives. No jail term, but Mitchell would lose his allowance for a month, and his father would get a full report when they returned to North Carolina.

After the lecture was over, even Aunt George was unusually quiet, but Allyn did notice that she was trying very very especially hard not to let herself smile.

Thatched Cottage, County Limerick

The Castle Catastrophe

Ireland! Allyn was deliriously happy. They passed through the passport check and put all the luggage on two giant carts. When they got to the money-exchange desk, Mitchell was surprised at the different sizes and colors.

"Look at this, Al! It looks like play money. Are you sure it'll buy stuff?"

"Yes, Mitchell," Allyn answered maturely. "Every country has its own money. Other countries don't care about George Washington or bald eagles. They think monks and queens and dictators are more important."

"What's all this writing, Mom?" asked Mitchell.

"That's Gaelic, sweetheart. In Ireland, everyone

speaks English, but some people can speak Gaelic, too," answered Mrs. Gallagher, looking around for her sister. "Allyn, did George tell you where she was going with the other cart?"

"She's getting the rental car key, and she said she'd meet us in the map shop."

The tourist shop was huge, with an opening big enough to leave a cart in the doorway and keep an eye on the luggage. Mitchell looked at the plastic trinkets, and Allyn went to one corner where she found books about places they'd be seeing. She stooped close to the ground and looked at a book about Bunratty Castle, and then two men close by began whispering.

"Thought you wouldn't make it," said one.

"Getting the rental took longer," the second man answered. "Some tourist lady tried to talk my ear off."

"It's set," said the first. "Here's the list. I'm planting a copy for Caloran. No fax or computer links. Too risky. He'll get it later. I can't be seen with him, but he'll send the contacts. I'll tell you the rest there."

"Where the devil is this place?"

"Moher Cliffs. The white boulder — up a short distance on the path. Tomorrow morning, 9:30."

"Cops?"

"We won't be followed," whispered the first man. "The gardai have no idea what's going on. The Cliffs are perfect. Two tourists."

"Hey, wait," whispered the second. "What about Loughshinny — is it still 'go'?"

"No change. It's too late now, anyway. You know, Triad power," said the first even more quietly. "Paid the right people — New York, Swords, Loughshinny. No trouble with officials, believe me. Just don't be late tomorrow."

"You don't be late," said the second man angrily.

Allyn heard them leave. She hadn't moved; she had tried to breathe softly, too. The voices were American, but she never dared to peek. Whatever they were planning, they didn't want the cops to know.

What was "go" for Loughshinny, she wondered. She had read that Loughshinny was a little village where nothing much happened. The only reason her family was going there was because of the ... no. No, those men couldn't possibly have anything to do with the concert or Darryl James. The thought was so ridiculous that she felt like laughing.

Allyn tried to distract herself with color post-cards of Ireland, but the conversation bugged her. She was sure these men were planning something illegal, and she wondered if she should find a police-man and tell him what she had heard.

She replayed the conversation in her mind: Moher Cliffs, the white boulder, up a short distance, 9:30. There was something about not mailing a list to Cal — somebody. Tomorrow morning. Tomorrow morning at the Cliffs.

Aunt George was in the shop now, so it was time to head for their B-and-B in Limerick and for a good nap. It was already after 9:30 a.m. in Ireland, but it was 4:30 a.m. in North Carolina, which meant Allyn was too tired for anything like wild adventure.

As they piled everything into the rental car, Allyn decided to keep quiet about what she had heard in the map shop. She was already forming a plan — a plan her mother would spoil if she knew anything about it.

Outside it was a gorgeous day: sixty degrees and a deep blue sky. Allyn wasn't used to such crystal-clean air. America must have been like this a long time ago, she thought.

She and Mitchell were in the backseat, and Mitchell was getting more and more upset that they were riding on the wrong side of the road. "We're gonna crash, Aunt George! We'll get creamed on this side!"

"Don't worry, honey. Everybody thinks left here. The dangerous ones are the tourists, because they might forget and start driving on the right!" answered Aunt George, putting on the windshield wipers instead of the blinker.

It was a very short ride to Limerick, and the only tough part was driving around rotaries, which were called "roundabouts" in Ireland. It was hard for Aunt George to remember to circle left instead of right.

"There it is, George — Limerick Stay!" said Mrs. Gallagher. "Oh, look at the flowers!" There was a big garden in front of their bed-and-breakfast place, and it was packed with flowers: purple, yellow, red, coral, blue.

They unloaded the luggage, and then Mitchell insisted on being the one to knock on the door. "Mrs. Mahoney?"

"Oh, yes — the Gallaghers! I've been expectin' you! Please, please, come in," said Mrs. Mahoney with a thick Irish accent.

"Yep, that's us," said Mitchell," as he passed her and walked into the hallway with his bags.

"Hello! I'm Georgette Banks, and this is my sister, Elizabeth Gallagher. So good to finally meet you, Mrs. Mahoney."

"Yes, and certainly you must all be dead on your feet and wantin' some hot tea and biscuits!" said Mrs. Mahoney, as she led them to their rooms down the long hallway.

"I like her," Mitchell whispered to Allyn. For Mitchell, this was the supreme compliment.

Mrs. Mahoney made them feel right at home, but the rooms were a decorator's nightmare: two kinds of flowered wallpaper clashed wildly with the stripes in the curtains and the plaid in the bedspreads. Even Mitchell, who usually didn't notice anything about the decorating in a house, said, "Gee, Al, I thought she'd have a better-lookin' place."

"Maybe clashing is the *in* thing in Ireland now," replied Allyn, plopping on the bed closest to the bathroom. The bed felt so good that it was tough to make herself get a shower before changing into pajamas for a nap.

Aunt George had suggested that they take three hours for a nap so they would be wide awake for the big medieval banquet at Bunratty Castle at six o'clock. They felt like the fastest three hours of Allyn's life, because just after she shut her eyes, her mother was telling her it was mid-afternoon and time to do a little exploring in Limerick.

When they were all in the rental car again, Aunt George scouted for a place to get a snack. In the passenger seat, Mrs. Gallagher began reading aloud and telling them about the history of Limerick: "It was founded by the Danes in the ninth century, and — "

"Danes!" interrupted Mitchell. "Did the big dogs sniff it out or somethin'?"

"Not Great Danes, Mitchell!" Allyn told him. "Danes! Danes! Like Danish pastry! Like Danish furniture! You know, from Denmark."

Mitchell looked offended. "They ought to call 'em Denmarkans."

Mrs. Gallagher continued reading. ""A few hundred years before Christ, the Celts came to Ireland. They were fierce warriors with fair skin and red hair."

"Just like Allie and Aunt George," commented

Mitchell, trying to hold the pen between his nose and upper lip.

Allyn looked at Aunt George's bouncy hair. It was lighter and livelier than hers — like the sun when it's hanging around for those last few minutes on the horizon. "I bet Aunt George and I would have been great Celtic warriors," answered Allyn.

Aunt George laughed. "Warriors with *mercy*, Allie — we'll be a new breed."

"Mom, how tough were these Celt guys really?" asked Mitchell.

"Very tough!" answered his mother. "The Celts defeated the people who were living in Ireland, and all over the country they set up little kingdoms that were ruled by chieftains. The chieftains weren't the big shots, though. They were ruled by the regional kings. And finally, there was one High King, who lived in a special place called Tara in the north of Ireland."

"Durty Nelly's!" interrupted Aunt George. "Sounds good, huh?"

"Do you think they'll have soup?" asked Mrs. Gallagher.

"Oh sure, Liz. Everybody out!"

Allyn felt as if she had stepped into a time machine. Durty Nelly's, the village inn, was as old as the ships that brought Pilgrims to America, and she thought her wooden chair might turn into dust any minute.

Allyn closed her eyes and imagined that she was back in 1620, wearing a Pilgrim dress and riding side-saddle on her way to Durty Nelly's. Her dress was flying in the wind, and she wondered if tights had been invented yet.

"Allie? Allie, your sandwich is here," said her mother.

The soup and bread were great, but several hours later, when it was time to leave for the banquet, Allyn felt like lunch was still partying in her stomach.

Huge stones towered in front of them. "Here we are! Bunratty Castle!" Aunt George said excitedly. "Ready for an authentic medieval banquet?"

"What does 'authentic' mean?" asked Mitchell, straining to see the very top of the castle.

"In this case, Mitchell, it means we'll be eating with our fingers," replied Aunt George.

"Great!" yelled Mitchell. "Knight style."

When they were crossing the drawbridge, though, Mitchell's enthusiasm dropped, and he said he was disappointed.

"Why, Mitchell?" his mother asked him.

"Just look at this moat, Mom! No crocodiles, no pirrhana fish."

"Cheer up, Mitch!" said Allyn. "Maybe there's still something pukey left in the dungeon."

"Maybe," he mumbled.

Inside the huge door were men and women

Bunratty Castle

The Great Hall – Bunratty Castle

dressed in medieval costumes, and Allyn felt like she had just stepped out of the 1990's again. There was one dress that she wanted to own. It was a deep blue velvet, and underneath there was a layer of stiff material that shone like real gold. "They should sell this medieval stuff in the *Spiegel Catalog*," Allyn whispered to her mother. "They'd make a bundle, Mom!"

The medieval people greeted Mitchell as "noble master," and the rest of them were "his three noble ladies." They were ushered into the Great Hall — an enormous room with thick wooden tables and benches. Allyn was sure King Arthur must have eaten there with his knights.

"Swords, Mom! Please! Just a quick look before it starts!" Mitchell was too excited to sit yet, so they took a peek at the rest of the castle.

They discovered that Bunratty Castle had been built in the 1400's by Sioda MacConmara. There were three levels inside: the dungeon (Mitchell's favorite) and officers' quarters were on the first; the Great Hall for banqueting was on the second; and the personal living quarters of the Earl of Thomond (who had owned the castle) were on the third. Allyn particularly liked "the hatch" in the Earl's bedroom: it was a hole in one of the stone walls, and it allowed the Earl of Thomond to spy on folks eating in the Great Hall.

The Hall filled with candlelight, and the banquet started. There were supposed to be four dinner courses of "finger food," and when the soup was served, Allyn wondered how she was going to scoop it in her palm. Maybe they would just have to lap it up like finely-dressed hound dogs, she thought.

Fortunately, at that moment the minstrel instructed everyone to do the sensible thing: to pick up the bowls and guzzle the soup like peasants.

Allyn thought the musical entertainment was great, but it was clear that Mitchell was bored and that he wanted to wander and get the "knightly feel" of the castle. Allyn was sure he was just pretending when he said he needed to use the bathroom.

Mrs. Gallagher led Mitchell as far as the steps of the third level, where the lavatory was, and then Mitchell insisted that his mother go back to the table and wait for him there. What followed was an episode of supreme embarrassment for Allyn and an evening Mrs. Gallagher said she would never forget.

Instead of the lavatory, Mitchell had gone into the Earl of Thomond's chamber and had perched himself beside "the hatch." When he strained to get a view of every part of the Hall below, something round—something rubbery, something with incredible bounciness—dropped out of his shirt pocket and down, down, down into the Great Hall below.

BOOM! The superball hit the marble floor and bounced all the way up, up to the ceiling and down — SMACK — on the floor again. The music stopped; the singing stopped; the people gasped and protected their heads. One of the male singers leapt to try to catch it, but too late! The ball went up again and down, down — BOOM — in the middle of one of the tables. A man lunged forward to grab it, knocked over his mug of mead, and ruined his wife's dress! Chaos! Up, up again soared the ball, and then the plunge — SPLAT! A plate of ribs, a huge silver plate of tasty ribs in the arms of a beautifully-gowned waitress spun out of her arms!

"Duck!" yelled a teenage boy, but it was useless. Ribs knocked over candles and mead; ribs destroyed dresses and white shirts and personal dignity!

For a few seconds, there was total shock. The singers didn't move. Someone said, "Ball from the ceiling," but no one could figure out exactly what had happened.

Mitchell, in the meantime, had rushed downstairs. He had tried to look like an innocent spectator, but Allyn guessed the truth.

While Mrs. Gallagher and Aunt George were helping a woman clean off her dress, Allyn pulled Mitchell away from the table. "It was you, wasn't it? Confess! It was your stupid superball, wasn't it? You brought it to Ireland, didn't you?"

"I didn't mean to do it, Al! I was just lookin' through the hatch, and it kinda fell out. Don't tell anybody, Al! The dungeon! Please, Al! I'll die in that thing!"

Mitchell was close to hysterics, and Allyn wasn't sure what to do. Humiliation, she thought. Here she was, trying to be the picture of sophistication, and her next-of-kin was a walking bomb.

The castle manager arrived a few minutes later, and he offered apologies and money for damaged clothing. For those who wanted to stay, he promised a new batch of ribs and an encore program of Irish history and music.

Allyn noticed that security guards had appeared, and they were looking for something— probably for the maniac who had dropped the super-ball. Allyn glanced at Mitchell, and Mitchell shook like a doomed man.

When the banquet was over, Mrs. Gallagher surprised all of them. "Mitchell, that was your superball, wasn't it?" she asked in a steady voice.

Mitchell's eyes filled with tears, and he nodded.

"I didn't want to embarrass your sister and Aunt Georgette in front of all these people, Mitchell, so I waited. But now it's time to talk to the manager." Mrs. Gallagher moved like a drill sergeant. She put her arm around Mitchell and led him quickly out of the Great Hall.

"What's going to happen to us?" Allyn asked her aunt, as the two followed her mother to the infor-mation desk. "Will they give us a 'family cell'?"

"Don't worry, Allie," said her Aunt George calm-ly. "I'm sure they have some kind of insurance for accidents."

The castle manager was a good listener, even though he was clearly upset. Mitchell explained his story between sobs, and the manager accepted the fact that the ball wasn't a prank. Mrs. Gallagher had to write a statement and sign it, and Aunt George signed something, too. Although the castle manager's tone and words were very courteous, he would have to mail a damage statement to them, and there *would* be a fine to pay.

Allyn winced; Mrs. Gallagher hung her head; and Mitchell kept crying.

Aunt George pulled them all aside and said, "Mitchell, I know you feel terrible, and I'm sure you'll be much more careful in the future. Won't you?"

Mitchell nodded hard enough to shake his head loose.

"Even after Marley's Ghost and this unforget-table banquet, I'm having the time of my life. I real-ly am!" insisted Aunt George. "But there's some-thing you can do for me. Liz, Allie, Mitchell — let's promise right now to put this evening behind us and to start out fresh tomorrow. Can we do that?"

All four of them looked at each other, and Mitchell did something unusual. He ran to Aunt George and hugged her tightly for almost an entire minute. Allyn could tell her mother was softening. She looked at Allyn, put her arm around her shoul-ders, and said, "We need to forget this, don't we, Allie?"

"Yeah, " said Allyn, glancing at Mitchell's tear-stained face.

With her arm around Mitchell, Mrs. Gallagher led him over the drawbridge. Allyn and Aunt George followed, and they put the castle and the Great Hall and the most embarrassing banquet of their lives behind them.

Mystery on the
Cliffs of Moher

Before going to bed, Allyn asked her mother if they could get to the Cliffs early — before all the tourists poured in. She reluctantly agreed that, if Allyn would take responsibility for getting everyone up, they would try to leave for the Cliffs a little after eight o'clock.

"Mitchell! Mitchell, wake up! We'll be late if we don't get going!"

"Wha—at? No school today, Al. Go back to sleep."

"Mitchell! Mitchell!" Noise wasn't working; she would have to be clever. "Mitch, it's a shame you'll miss breakfast. I'm too hungry to pass up those waffles and eggs and hash browns. Sorry. Maybe I can smuggle out a piece of bread for you. But don't worry — we'll stop for lunch in five or six hours."

Cliffs of Moher, County Clare

Like a blast of light, Mitchell jumped out of bed and headed for the bathroom. Success, thought Allyn. The next big challenge would be getting her mother up.

"Mom! Mom!" she whispered as she opened the door. Although Aunt George was already in the bathroom, her mother was still lying down with an expression of utter exhaustion on her face.

"Allie," she whispered, "I'm not alive enough to move. What time is it?"

"It's already 7:05, Mom. If we hurry, we can eat breakfast before 8:00."

"Allie, I'll do this today. But tomorrow we're sleeping later. Got it?"

"Yep."

In half an hour, everyone had showered in freezing water and had met in Mrs. Mahoney's dining room. It was like a miniature restaurant, with tiny separate tables set for breakfast. There were two strangers at another table, and Mrs. Mahoney was scurrying around like a waitress.

"Tea's hot. And will you be havin' coffee?" asked Mrs. Mahoney.

"Please!" said Aunt George, and Mrs. Gallagher nodded.

"Some juice then?" Mrs. Mahoney was looking at Allyn.

"Uh — yes, Ma'am," said Allyn. "Mrs. Mahoney, do you serve waffles?"

An Irish Breakfast

"Waffles? Oh, I don't, I'm afraid. But can I get you some wheatened brown bread?"

"Brown bread?"

"It's wonderful, Allie. I've had it before," interrupted Aunt George. "I think we'd all enjoy some, Mrs. Mahoney."

Allyn thought Irish breakfasts were very interesting. First, there was cold cereal, like an appetizer. Then came the eggs, Canadian-type bacon, sausage, broiled tomatoes, and thick "wheatened brown bread." When it was time to get up from breakfast, they all groaned; they had eaten a day's worth of food in half an hour.

When the luggage was in the car again, they said goodbye to Mrs. Mahoney.

"And you'll be gettin' a thrill today at the Cliffs, that's for sure!" said Mrs. Mahoney with enthusiasm. "You know the right roads then?"

"Yes, we've got good maps!" yelled Aunt George from the gate. "Thanks again for everything! Goodbye!"

The Moher Cliffs were northwest — past the River Shannon, past the international airport, and all the way out to the Atlantic Ocean. Ireland was an island, so most of the country was one big coastline. Allyn looked at the map again. To the south was the Celtic Sea, and beyond it was France; to the west and north was the big Atlantic; and to the east, between Ireland and England, was the Irish Sea.

What would happen at the Cliffs of Moher, she

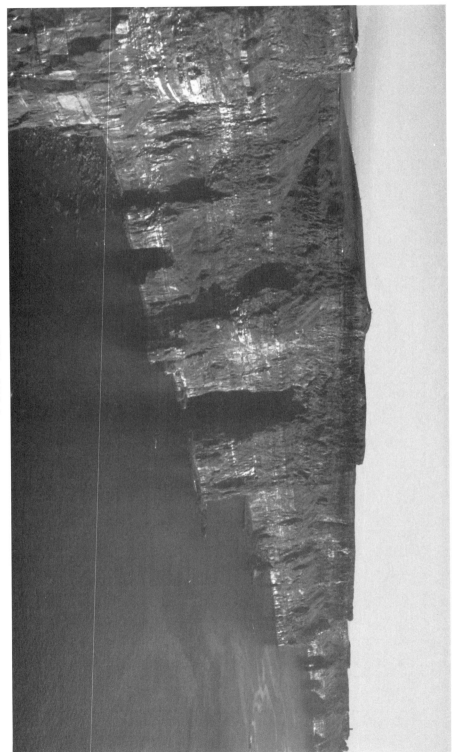

Cliffs of Moher

wondered. The men's conversation had been very strange. Maybe they were foreign spies who had fake American accents, or they were American mobsters, or they were C.I.A. guys working in Ireland on a secret mission — a mission they had to keep quiet from the Irish police, the gardai.

Finally, it was almost 9:20. Aunt George parked the car, and they climbed half a mile toward a scenic overlook that actually looked down on both the Cliffs and on the path that wound around the edge of the Cliffs. When they reached the overlook, Allyn was grateful for two things: for her good running shoes and for her backpack, in which she had stuck a camera, binoculars, writing pad, bottled water, chewing gum, and survival candy bar.

"Wow," said Mitchell, as he looked down over the miles of cliffs.

"Wow," echoed Mrs. Gallagher.

Below them were huge rock giants — standing in the powerful ocean, standing like an army, in a line that went on and on for five miles. The Cliffs dropped hundreds of feet, straight down, as if God had chopped off the ends with a huge knife. Green waves smashed against the bottoms, and every time the sun peeked out, it lit up white specks in the huge rock walls.

Allyn dropped her backpack and sat on the ground. For a few minutes, she just stared.

"Allie, we're going to climb the path along the Cliffs," her mother was saying.

Allyn looked at her watch: it was 9:35. The men must be there by now, she thought. "Mom, I really want to use the binoculars from here. It's the highest point, and I can see all the Cliffs. Can I join ya'll in a few minutes?"

"I don't want to leave you alone, Allie. There are a lot of tourists, and you just can't predict what kind of people might be here."

"I thought you said Ireland was safe!" protested Allyn.

"It's true, honey, and I do trust the Irish. But a tourist place like this is different."

Aunt Georgette and Mitchell turned and waved from the bottom of the overlook area.

"George, you and Mitchell go ahead!" yelled Mrs. Gallagher. "We'll catch up in a few minutes!" Mrs. Gallagher sat on a flat rock near Allyn.

"Thanks, Mom," said Allyn, as she got out the binoculars.

At first, it was hard to focus, but, incredibly, as she scanned the edge of the first cliff, she saw a large whitish boulder and two men at the base of it. She felt clumsy and unsteady, because the smallest movement made her lose them. Finally, with her knees steadying the binoculars, she could see the one man pounding his fist on the ground. When she focused on the other, he was using his hand to dig a hole in the soil. Allyn tried to keep the lens steady, but at that moment — at the worst possible moment in her entire life — she sneezed. "Ah-ah-ah-choo!"

"Need a tissue, Allie?"

"No, I've got some." Frantically, Allyn tried to get the focus back. It took too long to find them again, because when she found the boulder, the men were beginning to walk away. Oddly, they started down the path in the same direction but not together.

"I'm ready, Mom, if you want to go." Allyn stuffed the binoculars away and hopped up. "If we hurry, maybe we can catch Aunt George before they get very far."

"Okay, Allie, be patient. In fact, you'd better help your old mother up."

"Forty isn't old, Mom."

"That's the nicest thing you've said to me this trip!" said Mrs. Gallagher, and she put her arm around Allyn's shoulders. "Are you having a good time?"

"Yeah! Except maybe for Marley and the super-ball!"

Mrs. Gallagher laughed. "You have to say it sure hasn't been dull!"

Allyn smiled and nodded. "Mom, I was wondering, does the Republic of Ireland — not Northern Ireland — have anything that spies might be interested in?"

"Now that's an unusual question! I suppose they might, Allie — just because every nation keeps some things secret. But it's not on the continent, it's not a rich country, and it doesn't have much of a military. I don't think it's exactly a hotspot for spy activity!"

"I wondered, 'cause it seems like a great place for tourists, not for spies," said Allyn. She wanted to say more; she really wanted to tell her all about the men on the Cliffs and the conversation in the map shop. Allyn didn't like keeping secrets from her mother, because she usually needed her mother's help to figure things out.

Just then Allyn looked up, and there he was! One of the men! He was a few feet in front of her, and he never even looked at her as he passed. Then, not far behind, she spotted the other man walking more slowly. He was fairly young and handsome, and Allyn wondered which voice he had been: the first man, who had all the information, or the second one, who sounded angry and impatient.

"There they are, Allie. That's George's green bandana all the way up there — on top of the cliff."

When they reached the top, Mrs. Gallagher was panting. "You two are fast!" she said to Aunt George and Mitchell. "Let's stop here for a minute."

"Isn't it fantastic, Liz?"

"I'll say this much — you sure knew where to take us in Ireland," answered Mrs. Gallagher, resting on a low stone wall. The wall separated the path from about a twenty-five-foot area that ended at the dangerous edges of the Cliffs.

Close by was the whitish boulder, and Allyn had

a plan. "Mom, see that boulder? I'm gonna go take a picture, and I'll be right back."

The boulder was on the cliff side of the wall, but it was still almost twenty feet from the edge. Mrs. Gallagher cautioned Allyn about not getting anywhere near the edge. The men, however, had buried something on the west side of the high boulder — the side hidden from the path and nearest the cliff. Allyn knew she would have to explore there.

"I'll go with you!" Mitchell said with authority.

"No, Mitchell! I need to concentrate on my fabulous snapshot! I'll be right back." Allyn had already begun walking when she heard her Aunt Georgette explaining to Mitchell that his sister needed "space" sometimes.

When she reached the boulder, Allyn held up the camera and then moved slowly to a spot of ground that looked freshly dug. She knelt and told herself, "You shouldn't be doing this, Gallagher. This is none of your business."

As she was fighting with herself, her hand was digging furiously. "There!" She was holding a folded piece of notebook paper, and inside was a list of places and dates. Allyn got out her writing pad and quickly wrote seven of the eight addresses and dates before Mitchell's voice surprised her. Like lightning, she buried the paper and stuck the pad in her pocket.

"What's takin' you so long, Al?"

"Just trying to get a good shot, Mitch." Allyn waved to her mother and aunt. "Let's get back to the path," she said, pulling Mitchell away from the boulder.

For half an hour, the four of them followed the path over the Cliffs. Allyn tried to forget the paper and the map shop conversation, but both were pushing all other thoughts out of her brain. As she stared at the Atlantic Ocean, stretching out from the huge rocky coast of Ireland, a plan — an almost impossible plan — was shaping in her mind.

When it was time to turn back, Allyn had made a decision: she would include Mitchell. She would swear him to secrecy and use him as her investigative assistant.

Her second decision was to stop at the boulder on the way back and to take the buried paper with her. She was sure the paper had been left for a criminal — someone ready to help the first and second man do their illegal stuff in Ireland.

And *what* stuff was it? Only she, Allyn Lane Gallagher, stood between them and their diabolical plot!

"We'll see some old forts and megalithic tombs in the area," Mrs. Gallagher was saying, "and then we'll drop the bags in Doolin, eat, do some homework, and walk along the coast if the weather holds."

"Mom, can't we rent a pole for fishin'? Why can't I fish while you guys walk?" asked Mitchell, kicking a stone down the path.

Before Mrs. Gallagher could answer, Allyn interrupted, "Mom, I want to steady myself on the boulder again and get one more great shot before we go. I'll catch up with you in just a second!" Without waiting for a reply, Allyn raced up to the boulder. This time, though, Mitchell was running behind her.

"What's so special about this rock?" asked Mitchell, following her to the far side and disappearing from the view of the path.

"Hush, Mitchell! Just watch me," Allyn said impatiently as she dug for the paper. "I'm going to share something big with you, Mitch, and you've got to promise not to tell *anybody*. You've got to promise as though you're swearing with blood — understand?"

Mitchell nodded solemnly, and his eyes were full of respect.

"Where is it? It was right here! It was exactly right here, Mitch! Just a while ago!" Suddenly a bad thought made her uneasy. "Mitchell," she whispered, "I want you to stand and look around as though you're just looking at the scenery. But tell me if anybody's watching us, okay?"

"I don't see anybody lookin', Al. But Mom's comin'."

"Allie!" It was her mother, not far from the boulder. "Come on, you two! It's time to get back now."

"I'll tell you everything at the B-and-B," Allyn whispered, and she pulled Mitchell toward Mrs. Gallagher. "Sorry — we're ready now, Mom!"

On the way down, Allyn scanned for suspicious-looking guys. She guessed that whoever got the paper was not planning to stay and sightsee, though. What if someone had seen her find the paper and copy it? The thought made her shiver.

"Mom, if we feel like it, can we just chuck the itinerary some days and do something different and crazy?" Allyn asked, checking her backpack for more gum.

"Like fishin'!" added Mitchell.

"I don't know about fishing, Mitchell, but we don't always have to follow the plan. We've already got the lodging, so we need to plan our travel time, but that's it."

"Spontaneity makes it fun, Allie!" said Aunt George. "If we see something that looks interesting, we can make the time for it."

When they were in the car again, Allyn took out the notepad and glanced at the first address and date:

DOOLIN - BRUACH NA H'AILLE RESTAURANT

OCT. 9 - 6:30 P.M.

What could it mean, she wondered. Today was the ninth of October, and they were in Doolin. Her family was staying the night in the area, at a place called Aran-Scene House. Even now, Allyn shivered, but she just *had* to try out her plan. She would have to be there — at that very restaurant at exactly 6:30 p.m.

A Spy Itinerary

After seeing some very old tombs made out of huge slabs of rock, the family headed for Aran-Scene House, their next bed-and-breakfast place. Aunt George, in her typical lively style, was zipping along the roads as though she had been driving in Ireland for years.

"Aren't we going a little fast, George?" Mrs. Gallagher yelled over the roar of the engine.

"I get carried away!" Aunt George yelled back.

Allyn absolutely loved Aunt George's driving. The roads were curved and narrow as toothpicks, and the ride felt like being captive in the backseat of a rocket. Allyn and Mitchell stayed belted to the seat, but they gripped anything that would keep them from bobbing and bumping.

Soon they had reached the top of a hill, and Mrs. Gallagher exclaimed, "Oh, George! This place is gorgeous!"

Allyn got out of the car and thought she was in a fairytale. Aran-Scene House was a huge colorful mansion overlooking rocks and waves and the distant Aran Islands. As she stood at the top of the steep front yard, she realized why Ireland was such a strange and special place. It was modern enough to have indoor plumbing and cars, but it was so full of nature that being a tourist felt like pioneering on a wagon train.

"Neat! The islands!" said Mitchell with enthusiasm. "Let's go there!"

"Mitchell, I don't think we'll have time for the boat travel there and back," Aunt George answered him. "But I promise you we're going to have a great time doing some other things on this trip."

"A great choice, George," Mrs. Gallagher told her sister, as they were getting the luggage out of the car again.

"Todd and I stayed here, Liz, and I wanted to show it to you. Mrs. O'Dell is a bit different from Mrs. Mahoney — she's a little more firm and direct. But if a guest has a problem, she'll put herself out to fix it. She gets a lot of repeat business."

"This place really goes together better," Mitchell blurted out as they stepped into the big foyer.

Walking down the stairs, Mrs. O'Dell and her daughter heard the comment. "And were you expectin' a mess then?" asked Mrs. O'Dell with a teasing smile.

"Oh, no, Ma'am!" Mitchell said quickly. "It's just — uh — a lot nicer than our last place."

Mrs. O'Dell laughed and seemed to really enjoy this comment.

Aunt Georgette greeted her, and the two continued to talk while Mrs. O'Dell's daughter led Allyn, Mitchell, and Mrs. Gallagher to their rooms.

"Okay, Al! Spill it!" demanded Mitchell, shutting the door. "Mom's in her room, and nobody can hear you."

"Sit down, Mitchell," Allyn said gravely. "I'm about to involve you in what could be a dangerous underworld plot."

Mitchell was respectfully quiet, and Allyn described the clues she had gathered during the last two days. Finally, she said, "I should tell Mom. And I should probably give the list to the police, Mitch. But I want to go to that restaurant and see what I can find out. Even if I told the police all this, I bet they'd think it was just a game. Sometimes it's really lousy to be a kid."

"Al, what if somebody saw you dig that thing up at the boulder? What if the same guy's eating at this restaurant?"

"I know. That gives me the creeps, but I think

we'll be okay if we just watch for weird stuff — somebody following us or staring hard. If that happens, Mitchell, I won't be stupid! I'll go right to Mom, and Mom will go right to the police. And maybe the police will give us an armed escort, like a Sumo wrestler or a football jock, just to stick by us for the rest of the trip."

Allyn put the list in front of Mitchell. "Look at this *carefully*, Mitchell. I've got a brilliant plan."

Mitchell scanned the paper and looked confused. "I can't read your writing, Al. You should work on your penmanship."

Allyn could feel the impatience reddening her cheeks. "Mitchell ... Mitchell, I will try to be calm. I have excellent, EXCELLENT penmanship! I had to write this fast — FAST — do you understand?"

Mitchell nodded and kicked off his shoes.

"I will print this list neatly, Mitchell. NEATLY. And I want you to do something for me. Go to Mom's room and ask her for a copy of the itinerary, the sheet that tells us where we're going. I have something very important to show you."

Mitchell jumped up without a word and returned in a few minutes with the sheet. Using a page in her notebook (now her *spy* notebook), Allyn made two columns of dates and places and used a map to plot their trip.

Them	Us
<u>Oct. 10</u>: 3:00 — in Tralee, at Maherty's Pub	<u>Oct. 10</u>: in Salthill (too far from Tralee to spy on them)
<u>Oct. 11</u>: 4:00 — in Youghal, at Donovan's Pottery	<u>Oct. 11</u>: in Westport (too far from Youghal to spy on them)
<u>Oct. 12</u>: 3:00 — in Athlone, at the Ruin of Clonmacnoise	<u>Oct. 12</u>: in Boyle (too far away)
<u>Oct. 13</u>: Noon — in Drumcliffe, at Keanan's Groceries	<u>Oct. 13</u>: in Bundoran — Bingo! — Drumcliffe is on way to Bundoran (could spy there!)
<u>Oct. 14</u>: 4:00 — in Wexford, at McDyer's Pub	<u>Oct. 14</u>: in Kilcar (too far from Wexford to spy on them)
<u>Oct. 15</u>: 6:00 — in Downings, at Northview Restaurant	<u>Oct. 15</u>: in Ardara (too far from Downings to spy)

Them	Us
Oct. 16: nothing on this date	Oct. 16: in Burtonport
Oct. 17: 4:00—in Letterkenny, at St. Eunan's Cathedral	Oct. 17: in Rathmelton (1/2 hour from Letterkenny) Bingo!— could drive there and spy!
Oct. 18: ? —No time to get location!	Oct. 18: in Ballybofey
Oct. 19: ?	Oct. 19: in Loughshinny
Oct. 20: ?	Oct. 20: in Loughshinny
	Oct. 21: leave Ireland for home

"Do you see what this means, Mitch?"

"Not yet, Al."

"It means, my dear Mitchell, that we've got two chances to be where *they* will be. If we don't get any info tonight, we've still got a way to nab 'em."

"But, Al, how are we gonna get Mom to take us to that restaurant?"

"Ah — watch a pro at work," said Allyn, twirling her hair and flipping through one of the travel books. "Yes! Just as I suspected! It's here, Mitch —

recommendations, menus, description. We're in!" she shouted, and then rushed out the door to her mother's room.

"Mom, can I show you something in this travel book?" asked Allyn, plopping on her mother's bed and watching her hang up clothes.

"Sure. Why don't you read it to me, Allie?"

"Well, it's about this neat restaurant in town, and I thought maybe we could make reservations and eat there."

"What's it like?" asked Mrs. Gallagher, trying to decide what to leave in the suitcase.

"It's called *Bruach na h'Aille*. I don't know how you're s'posed to say it, but it means 'bank of the river.' The book says the food's great, and the prices are 'reasonable.'"

Mrs. Gallagher laughed at the word *reasonable*.

"What do you think, Mom?"

"I think we should ask your Aunt Georgette first. She might already have a restaurant in mind, Allie."

"Okay," she answered, and rushed out the door.

Aunt George was still talking with Mrs. O'Dell. Allyn stood in the foyer for a few seconds, not wanting to interrupt her aunt's conversation.

"Come and join us, Allie," said Aunt George.

"Thanks, but I just wanted to ask you something. I wondered if you'd mind if we went to a restaurant I found in my tourbook. It's got a real good recommendation."

"What's the name?"

Allyn looked at Mrs. O'Dell and felt self-conscious. "Uh, I can't pronounce it very well. I think it's Gaelic."

"In Ireland, we call the language *Irish*," said Mrs. O'Dell. "Can I see the name?"

Mrs. O'Dell glanced at the page and said something in Irish that sounded like singing, but Allyn didn't even try to repeat it. "Oh, that's a fine place. Fine," said Mrs. O'Dell with authority. "A good choice."

"Sounds good, Allie. I'll see if they'll take reservations."

"And you're welcome to call from the kitchen," said Mrs. O'Dell.

"Aunt George, do you think 6:30 would be a good time?"

"Fine with me, Allie. That should give us time for homework and some beach exploring," said Aunt George, as she opened the kitchen door.

Allyn raced up the stairs with a satisfying feeling of accomplishment. "It's set, Mitchell! It's a GO!" she told him and jumped on the bed.

"Great, Al, but we don't even know if the spies are gonna eat there. What if they just meet outside and give each other microfilm?"

Allyn looked at him and pondered this problem for a minute. Finally, she told him they would just have to improvise.

"But what does that mean, Al?" asked Mitchell, drawing space lizards on his notebook.

"My dearest Mitchell," said Allyn, strolling around the room with her hands behind her back, "improvising means flowing with the moment, using our keen detective minds to think of a plan *on the spot!* We shall be clever! Creative! No matter where these despicable men are, we need to invent a reason to be near them. Got it?"

"I think so," replied Mitchell, squinting at Allyn as though she were an impossible math problem.

"If they *do* eat dinner, Mitchell, you need to remember two things. One — we sit as close as possible to their table. Two — we make up some reason to be completely quiet so we can hear them."

"But, Al, who's gonna be there? If the list was for some *other* guy, then how are we gonna know what he looks like?"

Allyn stopped pacing. "Excellent question, Mitchell! What you'll need is a description of the two guys I saw. I will now write a detailed dossier for our suspects."

"What's a dah-see-ay?"

"A *dossier*, Mitchell, is a word you must become familiar with! We are detectives now, and we'll collect a file of information about each one of our suspects. The file's called a dossier."

Allyn wrote for a few minutes, then picked up the notebook, stood, and read as though she were giving a speech. "Listen carefully, Mitchell. Suspect A is very tall and thin with longish, straight sandy-brown hair. He's about thirty-five. Suspect B is more like Mom's height. He's very good-looking, has short black hair and a black moustache. He's probably about thirty. And they sound like Americans. If I spot either one, I'll get your attention, Mitch. And if neither one shows, we'll use our keen animal instincts to sniff out the criminal element."

Mitchell nodded submissively and continued drawing.

Allyn walked to the window and stared at the water and the distant pieces of island. "After tonight, we'll probably have to tell the police something. But first, Mitchell, I want ... RECOGNITION!"

Wisely ignoring this comment, Mitchell decided to perfect his enormous lizard tail.

"Mitchell," Allyn continued, "I want someone to say, 'There goes Allyn Lane Gallagher, teenage marvel. She cracked the code of the Irish spy network, and the Pope — deciding she *must* be a walking miracle — hung her hallowed portrait in the Vatican cafeteria.'"

Mitchell put his fingers in his ears.

Allyn smiled and pictured priests reverently kissing her portrait as they moved on through the ham-and-eggs line.

Mounting Clues

After exploring along the coast, Allyn and Mitchell were so distracted by the idea of spying that they almost forgot to change for dinner.

"Wow, Mitch, I better shower!" Allyn told him, and grabbed her dinner clothes. She ran down the long hall to the "shared" bathroom.

Fortunately, it wasn't already occupied. Allyn climbed into the shower and then yelled from the shock! It was ice cold! Finally, near the end of the shower, the water was just warm enough not to turn her skin blue, but Allyn wondered if the Irish were used to such cold water all the time. She decided that Ireland had bred a hearty kind of people. They all seemed to have bright pink cheeks, and they wore thin clothing even when October chilled up the mornings.

During the short ride to the restaurant, Allyn and Mitchell were completely silent. When they parked, Allyn scanned the area for her suspects, but neither one was in sight.

"What a beautiful old country house!" Mrs. Gallagher commented as they stepped inside.

There were flagstone floors, and Allyn could almost feel all the generations of Irish people that had lived there. They waited for the host, and a few seconds later, Allyn saw something that made her mouth go dry. He was there! Sitting at a table against the far wall was Suspect A, and a stranger was with him. Allyn had to think fast. "Uh, Mom, do you think we could sit at *that* table, away from the door? I'm kinda cold."

"It does get cold here when the sun goes down, doesn't it? I'll ask the host, Allie."

Mrs. Gallagher whispered her request to the host, and he led them to the right table — the table just two feet from the suspects.

Parallel but with their backs to the men, Allyn and Mitchell sat on one side of the rectangular table. The men's table was against the wall, and Suspect A was directly behind Allyn. The other man was closer to Mitchell. Although the seating was perfect, Allyn hoped it would be quiet enough in the restaurant to eavesdrop. Both Allyn and Mitchell had brought their notebooks and pens, and they left these open on the table as though they were spies waiting with a weapon ready.

Allyn was sure that Suspect A hadn't connected her with either the map shop or with the Moher Cliffs list. The Moher Cliffs was such a hot tourist spot that it wouldn't be unusual for Allyn to have been there *and* to be at the same restaurant in Doolin. Suspect A had hardly glanced her way when she sat down, and he seemed very involved in his conversation.

"Any suggestions, George?" asked Mrs. Gallagher as she scanned the menu.

"The seafood's a good bet. I think I'll try the mackerel."

Allyn and Mitchell were as quiet as marines at attention. They shielded their faces with menus and strained to pick up words from the other table. Allyn wanted her mother to be quiet, but Mrs. Gallagher seemed particularly lively and ready for conversation.

"What looks good to you, Allie?" asked her mother.

"I don't know, Mom. I think I need a few more quiet minutes to concentrate."

Her mother jumped right back into a conversation with Aunt Georgette, and Allyn strained to catch some phrases from the men behind her. She could hear Suspect A the best: "Payment's reasonable for how tough it is to get it through now. After this, we'll wait at least six months."

"And what will you be havin'?" the waitress was saying.

Allyn jerked down the menu. Her mother and aunt had ordered already. "Uh — uh — the same as my mom, please," answered Allyn, hoping her mother hadn't picked some mystery dish written in Irish — some surprise, like squid in peanut butter or eye-of-mackerel salad.

Mitchell asked for ravioli, which wasn't on the menu. Finally, after complaining about the selection and embarrassing everyone, he ordered "the same as Al."

Angling her open notebook against the side of the table, Allyn explained to her mother that she felt too tired to talk. She pretended to be drawing, but was listening carefully. The men were speaking in soft tones, but Allyn did overhear enough to fill half a page in her notebook.

"Caloran can't stop the drop," said Suspect A. "It's too late for that, but he can decide it's all going on the ferry. No involvement for you or the others. Of course, my employers get their money just the same — if not Ireland, then England."

Allyn hoped Mitchell was getting notes from the other man. She couldn't hear him quite as well, but she did catch two interesting phrases: "the pick-up" and "our British customers."

"This was an easy one!" said the waitress, arriving with four identical plates of mackerel, potatoes, and cabbage.

Allyn was incredibly relieved that her mother

hadn't ordered some Irish word for "pig brain." Now that the food had arrived, she hoped everyone would jam in the mackerel and not talk. After her mother and aunt had commented on how good the food was, there was enough quiet for Allyn to hear something that sent a chill up her back: "No, I don't think James knows. Maybe, but I doubt they trusted him enough to let him in."

Her mother picked *that* moment to ask her if she liked the mackerel.

Allyn nodded vigorously, hoping this would end the conversation. No such luck.

"Tomorrow," continued Mrs. Gallagher in a perky voice, "we'll be in Galway, and we can shop for little gifts to take back with us. Maybe even something small for Zack, Mitchell."

Zack Koslowski was Mitchell's best friend. To Allyn, Zack had as much appeal as roach droppings, but Mitchell thought he was a blast.

"Sounds good, Mom," answered Allyn. "Aren't you going to eat?"

"Sure, but I thought you'd both be excited about the shopping idea."

"We are excited, Mom. Terribly excited. Now I'm going to eat quietly."

Mrs. Gallagher looked puzzled, and she told her sister that they all needed to go to bed early that evening.

Too late! The men were leaving! Allyn tried to

eat and write anything else she could remember from the conversation.

"Allie, I think you should put the notebook away now and enjoy your dinner."

"I will, Mom. I like to write *impressions* of places. I try to capture my brilliant moments of inspiration exactly when they happen," explained Allyn.

Her aunt coughed and grabbed for a glass of water.

"Are you all right, George?" asked Mrs. Gallagher, patting her sister's back.

Aunt Georgette nodded, and a few seconds later said, "Allie, you're dangerous to listen to while I'm eating."

Allyn looked up and smiled, and then she leaned toward Mitchell to see how many notes he had taken. There was hardly any writing, and it was scribbled so badly that she couldn't tell it was English.

When dinner was over and they were back at Aran-Scene House, Allyn talked to Mitchell about the phrases he had heard, and she put all the clues together with her notes from the airport.

Mitchell read over the clues and then started building a tower with his clothes and other objects he was finding in the room.

"Are you thinking what I'm thinking, Mitchell?" asked Allyn, leaning against the back of her bed and staring at the colorful wallpaper.

"I'm thinking it's ammo," replied Mitchell in his combat voice. "They're droppin' off ammo for guys who don't want peace in Northern Ireland."

This thought had not occurred to Allyn, and she was quiet for a minute. "A very interesting deduction! Interesting, Mitchell," she told him and got up to pace around the room.

"What's a dee-duction?"

"Never mind," she said impatiently. "But I think it's drugs. They said they'd have to wait at least six months — probably between smuggling times in Ireland. I guess that could mean weapons and ammunition, but I think it would be a lot harder to smuggle in big things like that across the water. Besides, Mitch, you heard the word 'snow' from your guy. I know it's almost wintertime, but I betcha they were talking about drugs."

"But Mom said there isn't a big crime problem in Ireland," argued Mitchell, pretending his two pens were swords fighting around the tower.

"No, but maybe they're using Ireland to get drugs from South America to places in Europe. Fiona was upset that somebody was selling drugs in her town."

"Maybe," said Mitchell in a quieter voice. "Al, do you think we should just tell the cops now?"

"I'm worried about something, Mitch." Allyn lay back down on the bedspread and looked at the ceiling. "The men were talking about a man named 'James.' They weren't sure if 'James' was in on the deal or not. They talked as if the other contact guys didn't think they could trust him."

"So what's so bad?"

"Mitchell, it's right here in the notes. In the airport the men said something was still 'go' for Loughshinny. And now they mentioned 'James.' Don't you get it? *James* could be Darryl James! I guess it might just be some guy's first name, but it bugs me, Mitchell."

"Darryl James doesn't take drugs, Al. I've seen him on T.V., warnin' people not to start."

"I know that ... but sometimes people do weird things for money." Allyn was quiet for a minute and then added, "The point is, Mitchell, I don't want to tell the gardai until we know more."

"Which guards?"

"*Gardai*, Mitchell. It's in my tourbook. It's the Irish word for police. And *garda* means one policeman."

"Oh. Okay, Al, but I sure hope we don't botch things up just 'cause we're waitin' too long," said Mitchell, getting his pajamas and bathroom things. He pulled the door shut as he left for the bathroom.

Allyn didn't like it when Mitchell was right. She liked him best when he was immature or dense enough to be treated like plant life. It made her feel much more secure in her role as big sister. Tonight, as she lay absolutely still on the bedspread, she knew Mitchell had a good point. Even if Darryl

James *were* involved, it was a big mistake to try to protect him from getting caught. Selling or smuggling drugs hurt people — usually young people who didn't know any better — and anyone who did that deserved to go to jail.

Allyn could feel the tears forming. It was probably ridiculous to think the men were talking about Darryl James. It was probably ridiculous to think she knew anything about their plans.

Darryl James was her hero, like the way Mitchell felt about baseball stars. Heroes were hard to lose, and Allyn didn't want to lose Darryl James. She wiped her eyes and sat up. Not telling the police was risky, and she might regret it later. She couldn't have explained it to anyone, but something inside was prompting her to get as much information as she could before going to the gardai.

Allyn looked at the meeting times again. On Friday, October 13, there would be another contact meeting at Keanan's Groceries in Drumcliffe. She thought a grocery store was a very strange place for a meeting. As she looked at the list, Allyn noticed that all the places were either public or tourist spots, and maybe there was a good reason for that.

She would *have* to persuade her mother to stop in Drumcliffe on the way to Bundoran! As she stared at the towns listed, Allyn decided that either Suspect A and Suspect B were splitting up — one going north and the other south — or there were more people involved. The contact places were scattered all over Ireland, and no one man could do it alone.

Shutting the notebook and grabbing her pajamas, Allyn had a funny feeling in her stomach. She passed Mitchell in the hall and wondered if she were dragging him into something much too dangerous — so dangerous that it would change their lives forever.

Fiona and Her People

The next morning they were on their way to Galway. Allyn thought Mitchell was acting very strangely. One minute he pretended to be tough, and the next he was a worried little boy. They were passing notes to each other, and Mitchell's went from "Okay, Al, I can take danger" to "What if they try to kill us, Al?"

Aunt Georgette started talking about the two Ice Ages of Ireland, and Allyn was glad to stop the notes. "So what did the glaciers do again?" Allyn asked her.

"They left lots of lakes and boulders in Ireland as they retreated north. They also left a land bridge that connected Ireland to Great Britain," explained

Aunt George. "That's how the earliest settlers came to Ireland. They were able to walk over the land bridge."

"When was that?" asked Mitchell, looking a little more interested.

"About 6,000 B.C., honey. A long time ago."

"Before Mom was born," added Allyn, smiling.

Mrs. Gallagher turned around in the front seat. "Several years before."

"Why is it an island now?" asked Mitchell. "Did somebody blow up the bridge?"

"Well, Mitchell, it wasn't really a bridge — "

Allyn interrupted, "LAND BRIDGE, Mitchell! LAND! And they didn't even have dynamite!"

"Allie, hush," said Mrs. Gallagher. "Let Aunt George explain it."

Allyn folded her arms, sat back and realized she was impatient and irritable. She wasn't angry at Mitchell — even if he did ask stupid questions. She was angry at Darryl James. She had already convicted him in her mind and had pictured him playing his guitar in a jail cell. Allyn wanted him to be innocent so badly, but she was afraid she'd find out he was guilty of some bad crime. It was a strange thing, but when she got very afraid about something, she would act angry and impatient with her mother or Mitchell.

"And there are no snakes in Ireland, either," said Aunt George.

"Shucks," answered Mitchell. "How come?"

"The Irish have a legend about St. Patrick driving the snakes out of Ireland."

"Like with one of those huge bulldozers?" asked Mitchell, fascinated.

Allyn rolled her eyes and bit her tongue. She noticed her aunt was trying not to laugh.

"Not exactly, Mitchell," replied Aunt George, as though he had asked a sensible question. "I don't think they had bulldozers at the time. Saint Patrick was the man who brought the good news of Christianity to Ireland, and the Irish believe his work and blessing made the snakes flee the whole country. As the scientists would explain it, though, there are no snakes because Ireland was the last country in Europe to be covered in ice, so the snakes and the moles and the weasels are all gone."

"George, we want to get to N18. That's the primary road. The road we're on should take us there eventually," said Mrs. Gallagher, as she peered at the outstretched map.

Allyn was noticing less and less green outside. Then she was amazed that the landscape looked so strange and dead that it could have been another planet! There were hills and hills of nothing but rock.

The area was called "The Burren," and Mitchell insisted that they stop and get out of the car. They walked a little, and Aunt Georgette actually found

A dolmen (megalithic tomb) in The Burren

something alive — very tiny wildflowers growing around some of the rocks.

Allyn and Mitchell pretended their new names were A1 and A2. They were explorers from Alphabet Zulu, a planet light-years from a place called Earth. The people of Earth had been destroyed by a collision with a meteor. Nothing was left but tiny mutant wildflowers that would someday grow into big flowers with arms and legs and a scientific vocabulary.

When they were back in the car, Mitchell (A2) asked Allyn if mutant wildflowers would build their own spaceship and invade Alphabet Zulu.

"Probably not, A2," Allyn told him. "I think giant wildflowers would croak if they traveled for years cooped up in a spaceship with stale air and recycled manure."

The ride to Galway was going very fast because Allyn and Mitchell were making up lots of details about how mutant wildflowers would rule the earth. The rich ones would live in huge greenhouses with food fit for roses and gold-plated water sprinklers.

"Let's stop at a grocery store for lunch things, George," said Mrs. Gallagher. "I think we should eat before trying to shop anywhere."

The town of Galway was packed with people. It surprised Allyn because Ireland didn't seem very crowded at all. They had passed just a few cars on the roads.

In the middle of town, Mitchell spotted a bakery, but no one saw a grocery store. Even with a good map of Galway, Mrs. Gallagher was having trouble directing her sister out of the busy center and back toward the road to Salthill.

"Let's forget the groceries until we unpack at our B-and-B in Salthill," Mrs. Gallagher said finally. "But I think we need help getting back to the main road."

"Maybe that man would help us," suggested Mitchell, pointing toward an older man in a brown tweed jacket and cap.

"Good idea, Mitchell," answered Aunt George, pulling to the left curb.

Mrs. Gallagher was on the left, because the steering wheel in Irish cars was always on the right. She opened her window and said, "Uh — Sir, excuse me. I'm afraid we've gotten turned around somehow and we're lost. Would you know how we can get to Salthill from here?"

"Oh, Salthill," replied the man, taking off his cap and smoothing his thin white hair. "It's just a few miles from here. But you're goin' the wrong direction."

"We've had some trouble with the one-way streets," said Aunt George.

"Yes, well, I'm just out for a ramble today, and it would be easiest if I came along and showed you."

Allyn wasn't sure she understood. She thought

the man was asking to climb into the car to guide them out of the city.

"That's so kind of you," said Mrs. Gallagher, "but it would really take you out of your way."

"Oh, it's a fine day. Would make my ramble even nicer!" said the old stranger cheerfully.

Allyn's mother was looking at Aunt Georgette for help in making the decision. In the United States, Mrs. Gallagher never let strangers into the car.

Allyn saw her aunt wink reassuringly at her mother.

"Mitchell, move over into the middle, honey. I'm coming back there." Mrs. Gallagher grabbed her things and climbed into the backseat.

"He's coming with us?" asked Mitchell excitedly. "Neat!"

The man bent slowly and eased himself into the passenger seat. At first, Allyn wondered if he were either drunk or senile, because his directions seemed hard to follow. Soon, though, she realized that he had gotten them out of Galway much faster than it had taken to get tangled in it.

"I'll get out here then," he said happily.

"But you're at least three miles from where we saw you," Aunt Georgette said with a concerned face.

"And such a nice ride, too," said the man. "It makes a better ramble." He climbed out and added, "Good day to you then. You'll like bein' near the bay."

They all thanked him, and Allyn watched as he

moved at a good pace back toward Galway. The Irish were so different, she thought. She doubted that any American would go three miles out of his way to give directions. Allyn wondered if Fiona and her family did things like that.

"Mom, can I call Fiona from Bay House?"

"It's fine with me, Allie. But it'll be cheaper if we wait until tonight."

Allyn was much more excited about calling Fiona than shopping in Galway. She really liked Salthill, though. It was easy to spot Bay House, Mrs. Dineen's bed-and-breakfast place. It was a large, fancy house with a great view of Galway Bay.

Mrs. Dineen directed them to something called a "supermarket." It was nothing like an American supermarket! Mitchell was excited to see many American brand-names, but the place was like a tiny neighborhood grocery store that didn't have much food choice.

Sitting on benches right next to the bay, they picnicked with peanut butter, fresh bread, cheese, fruit, and bottled water. After lunch, Aunt George felt more confident about finding her way around Galway, so they returned to the city and shopped. Allyn had fun buying an Irish wool scarf, a music tape, and some little souvenirs.

On the way back to Bay House, though, Allyn stared at the music tape and thought of Darryl James. Allyn wished she had never overheard the talk in the airport and had never dug up the paper at the Cliffs. Maybe it was silly to think "James" and "Loughshinny" had anything to do with Darryl James's concert there, but she had that strange inner feeling again — the feeling that she should trust her intuition.

For dinner, they enjoyed Mrs. Dineen's hospitality at Bay House. She was a good cook, and she told Mrs. Gallagher that getting Fiona's phone number would be no problem and that she would help them make the long-distance call. In just the last three weeks, Allyn had written two long letters to Fiona, and she hoped they had gotten to Glengariff already.

Not long after dinner, Allyn was standing in the kitchen and waiting for a voice to answer her call to Fiona.

"Is this Mrs. O'Cleary?"

"Yes. Who is it?" Mrs. O'Cleary had such a strong Irish accent that Allyn had to strain to understand her.

"Uh, Allyn. Allyn Gallagher. I'm Fiona's penpal — from America. I'm in Ireland now, and I wondered if I could talk to Fiona." There was static on the line, and Allyn hoped she had heard.

"Yes! Yes," she said excitedly. "Just a moment then."

"Allyn?"

"Fiona? It's me! I'm in Salthill, near Galway."

"Yes, and thank you for your letters, Allyn!"

Fiona's voice had an older sound. "How do you like Ireland?"

"Oh, Fiona, it's great! We went to the Moher Cliffs, and we've stayed in people's houses, and we went to this neat medieval banquet in Bunratty Castle! I just wish we could go south and visit you."

"I do, too, Allyn. But I know it's miles from your way. Donegal is it you're goin' to next?"

"Well, Bundoran first and then north." Allyn was glad that her mother and Mrs. Dineen were talking and leaving the kitchen. "Fiona," she whispered, "can you still hear me?"

"Yes."

"Fiona, have the drugsellers been caught in your town?"

"I don't think so. Allyn, you're not thinkin' of takin' drugs are you?"

"No! Fiona, I heard some men planning to smuggle something into Ireland, and I think it might be drugs. They said something about Loughshinny, and I'm worried. I think maybe it's got something to do with Darryl James's concert."

"Allyn, go to the gardai! Please — tell them if you know something. The problem's been growin' here, and I'm worried about my sister Claire."

Allyn was quiet for a moment. "Fiona, I promise that if I find out Darryl James isn't involved, I'll go right to the police. I won't leave Ireland without letting someone know."

Fiona told Allyn that smugglers were dangerous

and that she needed to be very careful, and then Mrs. Gallagher peeked into the kitchen and motioned for Allyn to end her phone call.

"Fiona, I'll be in Loughshinny for the concert on the twentieth. I'll be in the first row. I know there's probably no way you could make it, but if you can, look for someone with hair that's kind of a dirty-red color, like a very old tomato. That's me. I'll be sitting next to a little boy with blond hair. And my mom's tall, with shoulder-length blondish hair, too."

"It would be a real miracle if I made it to that!" answered Fiona, and she laughed a little. "I'll be excited if I can get ten miles from Glengariff!"

It was hard to say goodbye, but Allyn was so happy that she'd finally heard Fiona's voice. It was low and much more soothing than Sally's. Sally had a bouncy personality, and Allyn could tell that Fiona was quieter. She wondered if people in Ireland grew up faster, because it was harder to survive here.

Ireland was a beautiful country, but there weren't many luxuries. Allyn was sure that people didn't have much money for vacations. It didn't seem fair that she could do so many things that Fiona couldn't afford. That night, lying in bed, Allyn remembered complaining to her mother about little things like not having a purse from a fancy store in New York—just because Sally had one.

Now she felt ashamed about it, and she wondered if *that's* what it felt like to grow up.

Danger in Drumcliffe

For the next few days there was a light steady rain, and Allyn and Mitchell were able to catch up on their homework. On Wednesday, October 11, they were in the far west, and mist covered the tops of rough rock-covered mountains. There were times when Allyn thought she was in a mysterious storybook place where everything was alive: the changing clouds, shadowy mountains, wild shade of the ocean, and miles and miles of shifting greens in the land.

Near the tiny village of Letterfrack, Aunt George stopped along the road and let an old woman and her small grandson ride with them. This woman had no car and was used to relying on hitchhiking. She was grateful for the ride into Letterfrack so she could buy groceries. Everything was "grand" to her — including answering all Mitchell's questions and bumping along in a tiny car with her grandson squirming on her lap!

Allyn thought the Irish must be the friendliest, most easygoing people in the world. She thought it was really a shame that most Americans had heard about the years of fighting in Northern Ireland but hadn't seen how all the peace-loving Irish lived.

The Republic of Ireland had warm people, and the "pace of living" seemed slow and peaceful. Now that she was getting to know the Irish, Allyn could understand what her mother had said about Northern Ireland, too. The night before they left on the trip, her mother had told Allyn that sometimes a small group of violent people can spoil the reputation of an entire country. After meeting the Irish in the Republic of Ireland, Allyn could imagine that most of the people in Northern Ireland had probably never wanted the violence — no matter what their politics were.

After driving north along the winding Atlantic coast, on Thursday the family headed east, toward the heart of Ireland — toward Lough Key Forest Park in Boyle. *Lough* was the Irish word for "lake."

When they finally pulled into the park, it was almost evening, but Mitchell asked Aunt George to take an "explorer hike" with him. Aunt George loved finding strange plants and creatures in the woods, so she was happy to oblige him.

Mrs. Gallagher wanted to write some postcards, so Allyn was glad she would have some quiet time in her own room while Mitchell was gone. She looked at the map and brainstormed about how to get her mother to stop in Drumcliffe at just the right time for Allyn to overhear the suspects. Although she planned the timing from figuring the kilometers and an average speed between Boyle and Drumcliffe, Allyn thought that overhearing information in a place like a grocery store would be impossible.

She checked her spy notebook again: *October 13, Drumcliffe, Keanan's Groceries, noon*. The only way to stop there would be to make up some reason why the family should picnic in Drumcliffe. Something had to work, because if Allyn missed this meeting, she wouldn't be close to any other meeting point until Letterkenny on October 17. It would be agony to wait for five days to find out if Darryl James was involved or not! Already the suspects had met in three places since the restaurant meeting in Doolin. She had missed all of them, and maybe she would miss tomorrow's meeting, too.

Allyn felt depressed, which meant she couldn't sleep that night. The room in their Forest Park B-and-B was cold and more barely furnished than the other places where they had stayed, and Allyn wished it were morning. Mitchell was asleep, and

Allyn turned on the light in the attached bathroom. She got out her spy notebook, sat on the bathroom rug, and looked over the dialogue details again. What in the world did "triad power" mean, she wondered. Allyn had written "triad power — Loughshinny officials," but she couldn't remember why she had written it. The notes were from the airport conversation, and Allyn was upset that she had completely forgotten everything that wasn't in her notes.

On Friday morning, Mitchell shook her arm and, two inches away from her ear, told her she had better get up.

"Mitch, this is cruel! Either you pasted my eyelids shut or I'm having a nightmare that it's morning already."

"It's no nightmare, Al. Get up or you're gonna miss breakfast."

"Mitchell," she whispered, "do you realize what day it is?"

"Friday. The day we try to get Mom to take us to Drumstick," said Mitchell calmly.

Allyn was still too groggy to laugh. "Drum*cliffe*, Mitchell. You have to watch for Keanan's Groceries. If you spot it, tap my leg or something. I've already got a plan to get us there. Mitch, go look at the description of Suspect B again in my notebook. You already know what Suspect A looks like. If you see either one in the grocery store, get my attention, okay? Just keep your eyes open for anything suspicious."

"You can't even *get* your eyes open, Al. Maybe I'll have to go to Drumstick alone."

Mitchell's comment was enough of a challenge to get Allyn out of bed and into the shower. She dressed quickly, because now she was anxious to see if her plan would work. She took her tourbook with her to breakfast and told her mother and aunt that she'd like to see William Butler Yeats's grave in Drumcliffe.

"You like Yeats, Allie?" asked Aunt George. "He's a very good poet, but I didn't want to drag you and Mitchell to the Yeats Museum in Sligo because I thought you'd be bored."

Allyn was in trouble. If they went to the Yeats Museum in Sligo first, there wouldn't be enough time to get to Keanan's Groceries in Drumcliffe at noon. She had to think fast.

"Uh, Aunt George, I really hate to ask you this, but do you think we could go to Yeats's grave instead of to the museum? Mitch would probably think it was less boring to creep into a cemetery than to see old yellow papers and poets' junk."

"Yeah. Less boring. I like tombs," said Mitchell.

Aunt George laughed. "I wouldn't mind that at all, Mitchell. I've never seen Yeats's tombstone."

In a short time, they had said goodbye to Mrs. Conroy, the owner of Forest Park House, and were on their way to Drumcliffe. Allyn thought it would be a miracle if she had planned the timing right. If the ride took too long, she'd suggest getting groceries and ice first, before seeing Yeats's grave. If they arrived an hour or more early, Allyn would have to be creative; she'd have to stall them.

Mitchell was behaving strangely again. Allyn knew that he was excited and scared at the same time. As they were riding, Mitchell was drawing a square building that he labeled "Grocery Store." He made the front door into a big mouth with fangs, and there was a long tongue rolling out of it, like a walkway.

"Sligo!" said Mrs. Gallagher. "George, maybe we should get fresh ice and lunch supplies here. There's probably a good selection."

Allyn and Mitchell looked at each other. They hadn't expected this problem. Allyn noticed that the sky had gotten cloudier, and it gave her an idea.

"Uh, Mom, I think it might rain soon. It would not be fun to see the grave in the rain, so could we just go on and maybe stop in Drumcliffe for food?"

"It does look a little like rain. You never know in Ireland," answered Aunt George. "I thought it would be a beautiful day."

Fortunately, Mrs. Gallagher agreed to wait until Drumcliffe, and Allyn leaned back and breathed a silent prayer of thanks. Another possible problem, though, was that the Sligo traffic was very heavy, and it might get them to Drumcliffe too late to see the grave first.

Allyn looked at the back of Aunt Georgette's head, bent in concentration as she tackled the traffic. Her aunt loved challenges, and in the middle of busy Sligo, she made progress with the insistence of a tank commander in an invasion.

Not far north of Sligo was the town of Drumcliffe, and it wasn't long before Allyn spotted Drumcliffe Bay. The town's main street followed the line of the coast.

Mitchell nudged her. There it was: Keanan's Groceries, on the ocean side of the street. It was 11:25 a.m., and, unbelievably, they were just five minutes later than Allyn's calculations.

"Drumcliffe Churchyard!" exclaimed Aunt George, pointing at a steeple in the distance.

"Are you sure that's the right one?" asked Mrs. Gallagher.

"Yep. You'll see," replied Aunt George, heading for the church.

Aunt George was right. They left the car and walked to look at the grave, and a strange chill went through Allyn. The damp Irish wind, the fast-moving, dark clouds, and the eerie message on the headstone all made her uneasy, as if supernatural things were happening all around her. The headstone message had been written by Yeats himself:

"Cast a cold Eye
On Life, on Death.
Horseman, pass by!"

Tombstone of William Butler Yeats, Sligo

As Aunt George began talking about Yeats, Allyn pictured ghostly horses and riders with huge bulging eyeballs. They were racing by the church-yard, pointing and sneering at Allyn as they gal-loped by. She shivered and completely forgot about the meeting at Keanan's.

Fortunately, Mitchell whispered, "Al, are we gonna be late?"

Allyn looked at her watch and nodded.

"Mom, I'm gettin' hungry," complained Mitchell. "We passed a grocery store back a few blocks. Can we go back and get some stuff?"

"That's a good idea, Mom," added Allyn. "Maybe we could have a picnic along Drumcliffe Bay before it starts to rain."

"I did see a lay-by," Mrs. Gallagher answered. A *lay-by* in Ireland was a place where people could park and sit by the ocean.

In a few minutes, they were headed for Keanan's Groceries. It was 12:03, and when they pulled in front of the store, there was no sign of either Suspect A or Suspect B. Inside, Allyn was surprised to see that there was only one other customer.

Someone was hammering and fixing a shelf. That noise and the music from a radio made it impossible to talk without shouting. Allyn told her mother what she wanted to eat, and then Mitchell and Allyn sat on the front step outside.

"Look, Mitch — that blue car is a rental. Maybe

the guys are here somewhere. There's a room behind the fish counter. Come on, let's check out the back windows."

There was a narrow gravel walkway between the grocery store and the drugstore beside it. What made the walkway even more narrow was a high row of stacked wooden crates. Mitchell followed Allyn, because they had to walk single-file.

As Allyn got close to the back edge of the building, she heard a familiar American voice. Quickly, she stopped and motioned to Mitchell to be quiet. Slowly and quietly, Allyn inched her way to the edge. On stone steps behind the grocery store, Suspect B and an unknown man sat facing the ocean and smoking.

"No phones and nothing on paper, you understand," said the stranger with an Irish accent. "If we change contacts, we'll let you know. The list — you burned your copy, I hope. Not for the gardai — it's INTERPOL we're watchin'."

"No, not yet. It was Gundersen who picked these stupid places. Tourist spots," said Suspect B in irritation. "If this operation croaks, I'm the one who has to answer to the Chinamen. They don't like failure, and I'm here to make sure Gundersen doesn't botch this thing. Listen — you're dealing with the big leagues, and your little network better be as good as Gundersen says it is."

"Burn the list, Mr. Fisher. I don't care what you

think of our organization here, but you better take my warnin' seriously. INTERPOL should never be underestimated," said the Irishman firmly.

"Just one more meeting, payment in Loughshinny, and I'm out of this stinking country."

"You and your associate will be grateful for this country, Mr. Fisher," answered the Irish contact. "Caloran is the best for reachin' any place in Europe. Contacts from South America, the Far East — they choose us for good reasons. We guarantee a safe ferry run. We get you an open door anywhere on the continent."

"Yeah, yeah," said the American impatiently, "so Dirk and his men slip into the dressing rooms, and half stays in Ireland."

"That's right. Only half on the ferry run this time."

"For English snowbirds, eh?" said Fisher, and he laughed at little.

"Yes ... and others," answered the Irishman. "Of course, we expect no problems, but if the airport authorities see more than instruments in those cases, Dirk will get word to you in Loughshinny. We do our best once it's out of the airport."

"Allie! Mitchell! Where are you?" It was Mrs. Gallagher's voice from the front of the building.

Allyn and Mitchell didn't answer, and in a few seconds the shop door clapped shut again. Unfortunately, instead of asking Allyn what he should do, Mitchell decided to let his mother know they were all right. Turning and running toward the front of the building, Mitchell slid on some gravel and fell!

Instantly, the men turned toward the walkway! They saw Allyn, dropped their cigarettes, and then darted toward her!

Mitchell was back on his feet fast and running around the front of the building. Amazing herself, Allyn did something brilliant. She pulled down a stack of crates, and it gave her and Mitchell just enough time to race to an alleyway on the other side of the building and to hide behind some trash cans.

Allyn's heart was pounding so hard she thought she would faint. "If Mom comes out again, not one word!" she whispered to Mitchell. "Don't even breathe!"

Mitchell nodded with tears in his eyes. He looked petrified.

There wasn't much of a view from their tiny alleyway, and Allyn had no idea where the men were. The family's rental car was close. Allyn could see the back bumper, but it was too dangerous to try to run to it.

Allyn hoped the men would just leave and assume she and Mitchell were Irish kids playing an innocent game. Just then, she saw the Irishman! He was walking into the alleyway! She took Mitchell's hand and squeezed it. There were loud

steps — closer and closer. Mitchell's face was white with terror.

Allyn looked at him and realized how much she loved having a brother. She loved him dearly.

"Shaunessey!" It was Fisher's voice.

Allyn heard steps retreating toward the alley entrance.

"I see a boy up the street. I think it might be the other one, but the girl's gone."

"Come on! We don't know how much they heard!" warned the Irishman.

Allyn knew they had to act fast! She motioned to Mitchell, and they moved quickly to the alley entrance. She peeked and saw the men walking rapidly up the street. Allyn and Mitchell darted for the far side of their rental car, crouched, opened the door, and slid into the backseat. Allyn had never been so grateful that she had forgotten to lock the door.

They crouched below the windows, but Allyn looked once to see if the men were still up the street. She hoped that whatever "little boy" they were talking about would be too fast to be caught.

Allyn was in Mitchell's seat, on the far left, and she saw her mother and aunt leaving the grocery store with a bag of food. Allyn waved both arms so her mother wouldn't call them. Then, when her mother got close to the car, Allyn put her finger to her mouth in a "don't say anything" gesture.

Mrs. Gallagher opened her door and whispered, "If you're just trying to hide from your aunt, she's spotted you already."

Allyn glanced at the blue rental car in front of them and shivered. On the sidewalk, the men were returning, and she hoped they hadn't heard her mother.

Mrs. Gallagher shut her door, and Allyn slid down even further. Mitchell, still terrified, had stayed low the whole time. Allyn felt so grateful when her aunt got in and shut her door before saying anything to them.

Start the car *fast*, thought Allyn. *Please*! "Aunt George," she whispered, "don't turn around, but get us out of here! We're playing 'secret agent,' and we're about to be killed!"

Aunt George loved playing along with a game, and she didn't disappoint them. She started the car fast and pulled out with a jerk. Unfortunately, it did draw attention to the car, and when Allyn peeked carefully, she saw the men staring toward the car as it moved up the street. The good news, however, was that Fisher and Shaunessey weren't suspicious enough to hop into the other car and chase them.

Allyn tapped Mitchell on the shoulder to let him know he could sit up. She had never seen him look so bad. For some reason, her eyes filled with tears, and she did a strange thing. She put her arm around Mitchell, pulled him close, and whispered, "You're the best brother anyone could ever want."

Puzzling Pieces

The picnic lay-by was just a few blocks away, on the same street as Keanan's Groceries. Aunt George pulled off the road, and Allyn wondered if the men weren't far behind. Mitchell looked as if he would never get out of the car again, and Allyn had to think of a safe way to picnic without being seen from the road.

There were no tables. The lay-by was a "scenic overlook" with a great view of the ocean. There was a stone wall surrounding the flat area where people could park their cars. Aunt George's idea was to sit on the stone wall and eat. There was no danger, because, instead of a sharp cliff, the wall was low, and lots of stones made a gradual slope down to the ocean.

From her list of contact-meeting places, Allyn
thought that Fisher (Suspect B) would probably be
passing them soon, on his way north, traveling
toward Downings. Mitchell, to be absolutely safe,
had slid low in the seat again, and Mrs. Gallagher
said that he needed to forget being a secret agent
long enough to eat lunch.

When Aunt George and Mrs. Gallagher carried
out the supplies for lunch, Allyn whispered, "Mitch,
it'll be okay. We'll sit behind the wall, on the rocks.
Nobody will see us there. Honest." Allyn squeezed
Mitchell's hand, and he nodded that he would try it.

Just to be safe, Allyn and Mitchell darted for the
wall and leapt over it fast. As they ate, they stayed
low enough that the wall shielded them from passing cars. If Fisher drove by, he would see nothing
but two women sitting on the wall and picnicking.

Allyn had taken her spy notebook out of the car,
and she was anxious to get as many facts on paper
as she could remember. As she ate a cheese sandwich, Allyn tried to relax her mind. She did her best,
but the list of notes wasn't very long:

Gundersen= Suspect A   Fisher= Suspect B
Shaunessey= Irish contact in Drumcliffe
Airport — shouldn't see more than instruments
          in cases
Chinese men who don't like failure — sent Fisher
          to check up on Gundersen's plan
Payment in Loughshinny for Fisher

English snowbirds
Shaunessey worried about Interpull (or Interpole), but not the gardai

When the picnic was over and the family headed for Bundoran, Allyn passed her notebook to Mitchell. He had calmed down, but in the notebook he wrote that he hadn't been close enough to hear what the men said in Drumcliffe. Allyn's notes would have to be enough.

They arrived at Mrs. McGee's, their bed-and-breakfast in Bundoran, just before it started to rain hard. It was mid-afternoon, but all of them were tired enough to want to relax for an hour before wandering around Bundoran. Mitchell had been so shaken by the chase that he was actually lying down to take a short nap. Allyn got out her spy notebook and decided to put all her little pieces of information into categories so the puzzle would be easier.

Info about Americans	Info about Contacts
1. Gundersen: left list of contact places; his bosses sent Fisher to check up on him; his bosses get their payment in Ireland or maybe England	1. Caloran: big Irish boss who has lots of contacts for smuggling things through Ireland; he can't stop "the drop" but can put all smuggled things on ferry to leave Ireland

2. Fisher: his bosses are Chinese men who don't like failure; <u>He would recognize me now!</u>

2. Doolin Contact: said "James" probably doesn't know about plan

3. Shaunessey (Drum. Contact): said airport people might see more than instruments in cases; warned Fisher about Interpull

<u>Info about Loughshinny</u>
Too late to change whatever's going to happen there; Fisher picks up payment there; "triad power" in Loughshinny

<u>Info about "The Drop"</u>
Reasonable payment for Gundersen, Fisher, and whoever bosses are (Chinese); must wait 6 months before trying another smuggling operation (drop); even Caloran can't stop drop now; if all smuggled things go on ferry, though, Irish network won't be involved anymore; drop is probably "snow" (drugs) because talked about English snowbirds (English people who use drugs)

Questions
1. What is triad power?
2. Who are the bosses/men from China?
3. What James are they talking about?
4. What is Interpull/Interpole?

Allyn read her list four times. Then she looked at the little village of Loughshinny on a detailed map of the east coast of Ireland. The map showed eastern ports where ferries left for England, Wales, and Calais in France. In her tourbook, Allyn read the small paragraph about Loughshinny again. Loughshinny was mentioned because there was a big carnival held there every August. Allyn guessed that Darryl James's concert was being held on the vacant carnival grounds.

When Mitchell started moving around and rubbing his eyes, Allyn told him she thought she understood how they were going to smuggle drugs into Ireland.

"Are you sure?" asked Mitchell, sitting up and leaning against the back of the bed.

"No ... I'd have to hear more stuff to be sure. But I think, Mitch, that 'the drop' — the place where they give the smuggled goods to somebody else — has got to be in Loughshinny, and the only unusual thing about Loughshinny is the concert. Shaunessey, that Irish guy in Drumcliffe, said that he didn't want airport people to see more than instruments in 'cases.' Mitchell, the cases must be the band cases.

And the band cases have got to be Darryl James's back-up band. They'll try to smuggle the drugs in their band cases from the U.S. here, and then they'll pass on the drugs to Caloran's guys in Loughshinny." Allyn had to stop because she thought she was going to cry.

"Maybe there's some other band, Al," said Mitchell with unusual sensitivity.

Allyn was quiet for a minute, and then she said, "Somehow I knew there was a connection right from the beginning, Mitch — from that talk in the airport when they mentioned Loughshinny. Then in the restaurant in Doolin I knew it wasn't somebody's first name. I knew they meant Darryl James."

Allyn got up, folded her arms against the window, and stared down at the wet flowers in the garden below. "What I don't know, Mitch, is whether or not Darryl James knows this stuff is going on." She couldn't say any more; tears were blocking the words. She started to cry so hard that it was embarrassing, but she couldn't stop.

There was a hand patting Allyn's back gently and saying, "It's okay, Al. It's gonna be okay, Al. I love you, Al."

Of course, this made her cry even harder! She turned and hugged Mitchell, and then sat on the edge of her bed and used a tissue to dry her wet face.

"Al, one thing that's good is that it wasn't Darryl James's idea. The guy didn't know if the others had 'let James in on it,' remember? So at least he's not that crummy."

Mitchell's point did help her to stop crying. She threw away the tissue and picked up her pen again.

"But how are they gettin' it through the cops and stuff at the airport?" asked Mitchell. They even checked *my* bag, and I'm nine. For part of the time, I put Marley in my jacket pocket in the special glass jar with the holes. I knew they might check bags for bombs and spy stuff. But then I wanted to let him run around in the carry-bag."

"I wondered how you got Marley through!" exclaimed Allyn. "Mitch, I need more information about who's really behind this deal. Gundersen and Fisher work for other people, and these bosses might live in China instead of the U.S. I have a feeling this thing is BIG, Mitchell. I don't think just a few guys decided to do some smuggling. If these Chinese guys are powerful, maybe they had a way to get the instruments out of New York without stopping at any checkpoints. Also, I read somewhere that Darryl James has got a private jet, so maybe that helps to smuggle it in, too."

"Maybe we should tell Mom and go to the cops now," said Mitchell, looking at her with a worried expression.

"I know, I know, Mitch. It's crazy to wait," answered Allyn. "If Darryl James knows, then he deserves to go to jail. But, Mitchell, if he doesn't know anything, and the police find out about this, they'll never believe him — they'll never believe he was innocent. That would just kill me!"

"But, Al, how are we gonna find out any more? Will it really help to wait?"

"We've got one more chance, Mitchell — the church in Letterkenny."

"Weird place for a meeting, Al. Do you think the priest's a contact?" asked Mitchell, as he pulled an anteater drawing out of his art folder.

"I don't think so, Mitch. I think they chose this big cathedral because it's a hot tourist spot." Allyn looked at the spy list once more, and she realized there was another problem. "Mitchell, this is bad! I don't know when Darryl James is supposed to land in Ireland. Maybe we'll get into Loughshinny one day before he does, or maybe we'll be too late to stop anything!"

"The concert's a big deal here, isn't it, Al? Maybe they'd tell us in the newspaper."

Allyn looked at Mitchell and decided that there were times Mitchell transcended the size of his own brain. This was one of those moments.

Television. Allyn remembered that American television cameras were coming to film the concert, and it made sense that Irish newspapers would probably mention details about such a big event.

"We need to get a Dublin paper, Mitch. I bet it's too soon to find anything about the concert yet, but we need to check a Dublin paper every day now."

"Okay," replied Mitchell absently. He was focusing on his picture of soldier ants throwing spears at the anteater.

Allyn got out her map of the eastern coast of Ireland, and looked at the ferry ports again. One was far to the south, many hours from Loughshinny or Dublin; but the other ferry port was called *Dun Laoghaire* in Dublin. There were ferries that traveled from Northern Ireland, too, but Allyn didn't know if Caloran and his men would choose Belfast, Northern Ireland, to ship drugs to England. If part of "the drop" was going on a ferry, maybe it was going from the Dun Laoghaire port in Dublin.

The ferries were ships that traveled between Ireland and Great Britain and between Ireland and France. In her tourbook, Allyn had read that many ferries traveled overnight, and they provided food and entertainment for the passengers. The ferries had several floors inside, so they could seat a large number of people.

"I'll be right back," she told Mitchell, got out her tiny notepad, and took it with her to her mother's room.

Aunt George was enthusiastically reading her Donegal tourist information to Allyn's mother, who was rearranging things in her luggage. "Hi, sweetheart. Come on in, " said Aunt George, seeing Allyn in the doorway.

"I've got a weird question," Allyn told them.

Mrs. Gallagher laughed and said, "That doesn't surprise us, Allie."

"Okay — I heard two words a while ago, and I don't know what they mean," explained Allyn. "One was *triad*. What does it mean?"

"Hmmm ... that's a toughie," replied Aunt George. "Well, 'tri' means three, so a triad might be three people who are involved in something together — maybe who have decided to work together."

"It's a chemistry term, too, Allie," her mother added. "I think it means three elements that are related, but I'd really have to look it up."

Allyn wrote her aunt's explanation, but she wondered if Gundersen had meant "drug power" and if triad meant three elements in a drug. It was still confusing.

"Uh — *Interpull* or *Interpole* is the other word," said Allyn.

"Wow, George, I need your help!" answered Mrs. Gallagher. "It stands for 'International Criminal Police,' doesn't it?"

"Yeah, Liz, but I don't know much about it," replied Aunt George. "I think there are lots of countries involved, and they investigate criminals with international reputations. One thing — it's all caps, Allie, like an abbreviation. INTERPOL."

"I think INTERPOL has its headquarters in

Paris, Allie. Where did you hear about it?" asked Mrs. Gallagher.

Allyn hated to lie; it always made her feel cold inside. Today, though, she was desperate. "Uh, it was a while ago, on some show," she answered. "I guess I'll go do my homework now. Thanks." She left the room without waiting for a response, shut the door of her own room, and leaned against it for a minute to let her heart slow down.

"What's wrong, Al?"

"Nothing, Mitch. Just go back to your homework," answered Allyn, as she walked to her bed and began putting her notebook and tourist information in a pile on the floor.

Allyn lay on her bed, closed her eyes, and thought about the risk she was taking. If the smugglers got away, they would continue to hurt vulnerable kids like Fiona's sister. She was sure that Caloran and his group were spreading illegal drugs around Ireland. *Snow*, the word Mitchell had heard in the restaurant, was slang for cocaine, a drug that got people hooked and could kill them. Allyn didn't understand why some people would hurt teenagers just to make money. She never wanted to love money that much.

If she went to the gardai now, Darryl James might be arrested, but at least the band's instrument cases would be searched and the drugs might be found. Allyn asked herself if Darryl James was really worth the risk of waiting with such dangerous information.

The rain had stopped, and Allyn heard her mother's voice from the doorway. It was time to explore Bundoran. Allyn felt too confused to enjoy anything, and she moved off the bed as slowly as a gnat in peanut butter.

Inside her, there was a weight — a decision so big that it was getting heavier and heavier. There wasn't much time left, and if she waited too long to tell the gardai, people all over Ireland would suffer for it.

Folk Village, County Donegal

Introducing Donegal

By the next morning, Allyn had made a decision. She wanted the gardai to catch Caloran and his Irish contacts *with* the smuggled drugs. Allyn thought it would be bad if the New York police or INTERPOL people found the drugs before Darryl James's jet left for Ireland. If the band members didn't get the chance to pass on the smuggled drugs in Loughshinny, then the gardai wouldn't be able to find or to convict Caloran and his Irish crime network.

Allyn knew that her love for Darryl James was probably interfering with the sensible part of her brain, but she decided to keep quiet about her spy notes until she had more information about Darryl James's guilt or innocence. It seemed impossible

Burtonport

Downings
Rathmelton
Letterkenny

Donegal County

Ardara   Ballybofey

Kilcar
Killybegs
• Donegal
• Ballyshannon
• Bundoran

• Drumcliffe

NORTHERN
IRELAND

REPUBLIC
OF IRELAND

that she would get any more details about him, but she had to try.

If Darryl James was innocent, Allyn wanted to make sure the gardai knew it. It was Saturday, October 14, and tomorrow there would be a contact meeting in Downings. Allyn was upset that Downings was too far away from them and that she would have to wait until Tuesday, October 17, in Letterkenny, to find out more information.

As they entered the town of Ballyshannon, Allyn was deep in thought and unconsciously pressed her nails into her arm so hard that they left a constellation of half-moon marks.

"We're going to meet someone special here!" announced Aunt George.

Allyn and Mitchell looked at each other. "Maybe Irish movie stars live here," whispered Mitchell.

"There it is! Connolly's Pub!" said Aunt George, pointing to an old tan building.

"Connolly" was the maiden name of both Mrs. Gallagher and Aunt Georgette, and Allyn thought it was funny to see the name on an Irish bar. Her mother didn't even drink alcohol; she had told Allyn that drinks affected her brain right away, so she had to stay away from them. Aunt Georgette liked wine sometimes, but Allyn rarely saw her drinking it.

Aunt George explained that, on her trip with Uncle Todd, she had met Seamus Michael Connolly, the pub owner and local historian. She said that meeting Seamus was one of the highlights of that trip.

They parked, and Allyn and Mitchell raced each other to the door of the pub. They opened the door, peeked in, and waited until Aunt George entered first. The pub was very dark, like liquor bars in the United States, but there was something friendly about it, too.

Seamus was alone in the pub, and he welcomed them warmly. "Hello! And isn't it a soft day, thank God."

"What's soft about it, Al?" whispered Mitchell.

"I don't know. Just nod and smile," she whispered back.

Allyn had never met anyone like Seamus. He seemed smart enough to know everything about Donegal, but some of his answers were so odd they were funny. For instance, her mother asked Seamus if he had been born "here." Seamus shook his head vigorously and said, "Oh no — not here! I was born two miles down the road!"

Seamus gave them all free soft drinks, and they sat at one of the wooden tables. Then, looking at Mitchell, Seamus waved his arms dramatically and recited a poem:

"Adieu to Ballyshanny, where I was bred and born;
Go where I may, I'll think of you
As sure as night and morn;
The kindly spot, the friendly town,

Where everyone is known
And not a face in all the place,
But partly seems my own;
There's not a house or window,
There's not a field or hill,
But East or West, in foreign lands,
I'll recollect them still.
I leave my warm heart with you
Tho' my back I'm forced to turn,
So adieu to Ballyshanny on the winding banks of Erne."

Mrs. Gallagher and Aunt Georgette applauded, and Mitchell, wide-eyed, asked, "Wow, did you write that?"

Seamus laughed. "Wouldn't Allingham himself be at my throat if I said I did! No, no, Mr. William Allingham, the bard of Donegal, wrote the verse. Sure, you've seen the bridge already?"

"The bridge in the middle of town, Mitchell," explained Aunt George. "It joins the two parts of Ballyshannon."

"Called Allingham's Bridge for the fine bard he was," added Seamus.

With the craziness of the smugglers and her sad feelings about Darryl James, Allyn had forgotten that Ireland was a *fun* place to be. Seamus was a good reminder.

Allyn and Mitchell climbed into the car again, and Mitchell rolled his window down to wave good-bye to Seamus. Seamus waved back and shouted something in Irish: "Go n-eiri an bothar leat!"

Aunt George began to pull away, and suddenly Mitchell stuck half his body out the window and yelled, "What does it mean?"

Allyn leaned toward Mitchell, grabbed his shirt to pull him in, and heard the faint answer from Seamus: "May the road rise with you!"

While Mitchell was getting a lecture about not hanging out of a moving car, Allyn was thinking about "The Pullins." Seamus had told them that there were limestone caves nearby called The Pullins, and inside them lived "the little people." Allyn had laughed when Mitchell asked his mother why midgets would want to live in caves.

When Seamus explained that "the little people" were leprechauns, Mitchell had gotten excited and asked his mother if they could sleep in a cave one night and talk with them. Now the lecture was over, and Mitchell was begging his mother again to get camping supplies so they could hide in The Pullins, capture one of the little people, and get a pot of gold to take back to America.

"With a pot of gold, Mom, you could buy a Mercedes!" argued Mitchell. You could start your own business — like a carwash or a motorcycle factory!"

It was hard to convince Mitchell that "the little people" were just a legend. Seamus had talked as though they were as real as the moon, and Allyn wondered if Seamus really *did* believe in leprechauns.

"We're in Donegal Town already," said Mrs. Gallagher. "Let's stop for lunch here, George."

"We gotta get a Dublin paper, Mitch," whispered Allyn.

After sandwiches at Carberry's Grill, Allyn spotted a newsstand, and then — right in front of her — was a wonderful picture of Darryl James! He was on the cover of an entertainment magazine. Inside, Allyn found a long article about the upcoming concert, and Mrs. Gallagher agreed to buy it.

Allyn couldn't concentrate on seeing Donegal Castle or any of the other sights in town, because she was so anxious to read the article. Finally, when they were back in the car, Allyn read every word carefully. The article said that Darryl James and his back-up band were scheduled to arrive in Ireland at Swords Airport, on the nineteenth of October at 7:45 p.m.

The night before, Allyn had studied her map to understand where Swords Airport was in relation to the little town of Loughshinny, and where they both were in relation to the big city of Dublin. Allyn's map was so cluttered with names and roads around Dublin that she had had trouble figuring the distance between Dublin and Swords Airport. Swords looked as though it was about ten miles north of the center of Dublin. Allyn decided that Loughshinny was about twenty miles northeast of Swords Airport. If Darryl James and his band planned to stay at a hotel in Loughshinny, they would be driving there after leaving Swords Airport, and it would probably take them at least thirty-five minutes.

Mrs. Gallagher had told Allyn that the family would arrive in Loughshinny sometime in the afternoon of the nineteenth. If the band passed on the drugs to Caloran's men in *Loughshinny*, then the time of the drug pick-up would probably be sometime after 8:30 p.m. *that night*, the night of the nineteenth. Allyn hoped that the Loughshinny gardai would have enough time to spoil the drug pick-up, because Allyn wouldn't be able to give them her notes until the afternoon of the nineteenth.

Maybe she was cutting it too close! Maybe she should tell her mother immediately and call the Loughshinny gardai from her bed-and-breakfast place *tonight*! As Allyn was thinking about telling everything to the Irish police, she remembered something important. "The dressing rooms!" she yelled.

Mrs. Gallagher turned around in the front seat and laughed. "Allie, we're driving through woods. Where do you see dressing rooms? For rabbits maybe?"

"Sorry, I was just reading and daydreaming about the concert, and I forgot where I was," explained Allyn, embarrassed.

The dressing rooms. Allyn remembered that, in Drumcliffe, Fisher had mentioned "dressing rooms." Amazingly, Allyn hadn't even written it in her notes; she hadn't remembered the detail until now.

Yes, she thought, the pick-up will be in the dressing rooms — dressing rooms for Darryl James and his band at the concert place! Allyn thought that there would probably be changing rooms backstage in the Loughshinny Carnival Arena, and that's where the concert was being held. The article had described the huge arena. It was just a few years old, and during the annual carnival, it was often used for big Irish theater productions because there was such a large stage. The only question now was *when*. Maybe there would be a rehearsal on the twentieth, before the concert, and Caloran's men would show up for the drugs. Or maybe the pick-up would be *during the concert*! With so many people and even television cameras there, the gardai wouldn't suspect that drug smugglers were working right under their noses!

And speaking of noses, Allyn had to hold hers because they were driving through the fishport of Killybegs, and it stunk! "Yuck! Let's get out of here, Mom!" she complained.

"It won't last long, Allie," her mother assured her.

Mitchell, of course, thought it was great. He forced himself to inhale deeply, and he made up a poem:

> *"Only fishermen like me*
> *Can stand to breathe the stinky sea!*
> *Girls like you and you and you*
> *Turn puke green, like oceans do!"*

After Mitchell had repeated this several times, Mrs. Gallagher suggested that he try making up a "nice" poem.

Allyn's reaction was stronger. She wanted to empty the litter bag into Mitchell's mouth. After all, she thought, with Mitchell's appetite, his mouth already understood garbage. With suppressed irritation, Allyn said dryly, "One thing's for sure, Mitchell. You aren't going to be the *second* bard of Donegal."

Aunt Georgette laughed loudly at this comment.

"Goodbye, Killybegs," said Mrs. Gallagher. "We'll remember you!"

Allyn was grateful to let go of her nose, and soon she was deep in thought again. She wondered if the band would set up the instruments on stage and then take the cases into the dressing rooms. The back-up band had five people, and they played guitars, banjos, and a drum. Darryl James was the only singer, and he played the guitar. Other than the drum case, the other instrument cases would probably fit in the dressing rooms.

Possibly the band would take the drugs out of the cases before the "roadies" set up the equipment and got the stage ready. Roadies were crew people who set up everything for concerts. The article had mentioned that three roadies were traveling with Darryl James and his band. For some reason, Allyn doubted that the band had let the roadies know about the smuggling deal. If the band hadn't even told Darryl James about the plan, then they probably hadn't let the roadies in on it, either. Each person that knew would have to get a cut of the profits, and Allyn thought that the band members were probably as greedy as they were stupid.

"Look!" exclaimed Mitchell.

"Time to get out with the cameras, gang!" said Mrs. Gallagher. In front of them were the Bunglass Cliffs — over 1,000 feet above the ocean.

Allyn was glad it was a clear day, because now, in the sun, the minerals in the Cliffs were like a rainbow: yellows and greens, whites and reds. Below, under a crowd of gliding seagulls, was deep blue water crashing against the tough rock. Ireland was so wild and beautiful that Allyn didn't want it to change one bit. If she could do something to keep ugly drugs and smugglers from polluting such a wonderful place, she would be happy — even if it meant losing Darryl James forever.

Allyn knew that, at that very moment, in the town of Wexford, in the south, there was a contact meeting. The thought made her shiver.

Already, it was Saturday, October 14, and the Letterkenny meeting would be at four o'clock on Tuesday, only three days away. Allyn would have to think of a plan to get the family into Letterkenny and at just the right time! She would absolutely *have* to—no matter what.

The Chase

For Allyn, the next two days were wonderful and terrible. Kilcar (or *Cill Charthaig*, as it was called in Irish), was a magical place, with deep-green rolling hills that looked over the wide expanse of sea.

Ardara, too, was fun but different. It was more of a market town. Aunt George bought a tweed coat, and Mitchell bought a little tweed cap "to look like the tough man I am." The fun part for Allyn was finding out how the Irish made tweed colors. They used plants and mosses that they boiled down with the wool into a dye. Heather made bright yellow; peat soot made a brown-yellow dye; and blackberry roots made brown. Then the plants could be mixed to make even more colors.

The terrible part of the last two days was that Allyn hadn't been able to think of a plan to get them to the Letterkenny contact meeting in St. Eunan's Cathedral. Even if they made it to the cathedral at just the right time, it would be hard to get away from her mother and aunt long enough to eavesdrop. Both finding the men and finding a place to overhear them seemed impossible, too.

"Burtonport!" said Aunt George, and she began talking about her time their with Uncle Todd.

Allyn wasn't listening. She was thinking about her father. If only her father were here, she thought, he would risk going to the cathedral himself and hiding to overhear the contacts. He would protect her and tell her how brilliant she was that she had figured it all out by herself!

Allyn's tears were streaming too fast to stop, and her mother glanced back at her. "Allie, what's wrong? What happened?"

"Oh — I shouldn't have talked about Todd so much," interrupted Aunt George.

"No, no, it's nothin' big. I just remembered a sad movie. Something I saw a long time ago." That was her second big lie in just the last week — not to mention keeping the whole plan from her mother. Allyn had a creepy, uneasy feeling inside.

"Want to talk about it?" asked Mrs. Gallagher.

"No, it's no big deal. I'm just kinda hungry," answered Allyn, looking out the window instead of at her mother.

"Who are those people?" asked Mitchell, pointing to a series of tiny mobile trailers, parked a little off the road in a field. There were clothes drying on lines, little children playing, and some old women sitting in folding chairs. "Are they part of the circus?"

Aunt George laughed. "No, honey. Maybe part of the *economic* circus. Ireland, like the United States, has some very poor people. They don't have homes, Mitchell. They live together in caravans that keep moving around the country, and they sell their wares, if they're lucky."

"Like gypsies?" Allyn asked.

"Similar, Allie, but most of these people are Irish. Here they call them 'traveling itinerants.'"

"I'm glad we have a house, Mom," commented Mitchell, straining for a last look at the traveling itinerants.

"I am, too, honey," said Mrs. Gallagher.

After picking up supplies for a picnic lunch, they all walked to a little cove-like area that had a sandy beach and was shielded from the strong wind. Today had been particularly windy, and Mitchell's new cap had blown off twice. Now the wind was ushering in dark clouds very quickly, and by the time they had set out everything for the picnic, rain began to pour. The downpour was fast and furious.

"I didn't expect this!" yelled Mrs. Gallagher. They packed up the food and rushed up the steep rocky hill that surrounded the cove.

Allyn and Mitchell reached the car first, and their clothes were completely soaked. Mrs. Gallagher and Aunt Georgette looked even worse when they finally climbed in with the food.

They drove straight to Mrs. Mundy's "Erin Place," their bed-and-breakfast in Burtonport, but Allyn was embarrassed when they arrived looking like sewer rats. Mrs. Mundy, however, didn't seem to mind that they were dripping rainwater all over her pretty rugs.

When she had dried and changed, Allyn put a pile of tourist information on her bed and read everything she could find about Letterkenny. Mitchell interrupted her once to ask if the traveling itinerants had heat in their trailers. She had asked him to be quiet, but it was a good question. She decided that Mitchell was turning into a decent human being after all.

Allyn turned a page in her tourbook, and a few seconds later, she shouted, "Yes! Yes, Mitchell! I've got it!"

She grabbed the book, tried out her idea on her mother and aunt, and returned to the room triumphant. "You may bow and call me 'brilliant' now, Mitchell."

"I won't bow to a nutcake," said Mitchell, blowing on his sneakers to try to dry them.

Allyn continued in her most queenly voice. "You'll eat those words, lowly Mitchell, for I — I,

Allyn Lane Gallagher, have done it again! Yes! We are going to Letterkenny to shop and to see St. Eunan's Cathedral! Letterkenny, dearest Mitchell, is the religious center of Donegal County, and Aunt George has never been there."

"So how are we gonna listen to the guys without them seeing us or Mom findin' out?"

Allyn was disgusted that Mitchell was asking the one thing she hadn't figured out yet. "Just forget it, Mitch!" she said in angry frustration. "And anyway, it won't be *we*. Just me. It's too dangerous after last time."

"I'm okay now, Al! I'm not scared anymore. Really!" Mitchell sounded desperate. "I can help! I'm smaller than you are — I can hide better!"

"I don't know, Mitch," she said quietly. "Let's just wait and see what it's like there."

Surprisingly, Mitchell didn't say any more about it. The next day, though, when they were driving into Letterkenny, he leaned toward Allyn and whispered in an earnest voice, "I *really* wanna do this, Al. I'll be a help. You'll see."

Against her better judgment, Allyn nodded that it was all right.

"Boy, I didn't think it would take us this long from Burtonport," she said to her mother and aunt. It's almost two o'clock."

"These little roads make it a lot longer," replied Aunt George. "We need to leave Letterkenny at least forty-five minutes before it gets dark — just to make sure we get to Rathmelton while I can still see the signs well."

"Can we shop before going to St. Eunan's?" asked Allyn. "It might take me a while to find something for Dad."

"That's fine with me, Allie," said her mother. "George, maybe we could get a Letterkenny street map from the tourist bureau. Let's look for the green bureau sign." All the tourist information places had a green sign in front that made them easy to locate.

It took twenty minutes just to get the map, to pick the right spot for shopping, and to park. Trying to plan her time right, Allyn waited until her mother and Aunt George had finished their shopping. Then, with twenty-five minutes to kill, Allyn faked ten more minutes of confusion about what to get her father. She had known immediately what gift she wanted: a brown tweed driving cap and scarf.

St. Eunan's wasn't far, and at 3:50 p.m., the four of them walked into the huge cathedral. It was a Tuesday afternoon, and the church sanctuary was almost empty. There was one old woman to the far right, sitting in the second row from the altar. At the very back of the church, in the last pew, was a young, muscular man with a tough look. He seemed somehow out of place in the pew. Although he was kneeling, his eyes were open and he was looking all around the church. Allyn noticed that just a few feet behind him was a marble information table and to the left of the table were steps leading up to a balcony, where there was an organ.

It was only three minutes before 4:00 p.m., and Allyn had to make a quick decision. The contact meeting might take place outside on the church grounds somewhere, and maybe she needed to think of a way to leave her mother and aunt and to watch from somewhere in the garden. When she looked again at the young man, however, he was watching the doors, and she was sure he was waiting for someone. Something inside Allyn persuaded her that he wasn't waiting for a priest.

"Aunt George," she whispered, "I bet there were Connollys in Letterkenny. Remember what the priest in Kilcar told you? He said that there might be Connolly family records in the Rathmelton area. Maybe you could check the parish records here."

"That's not a bad idea, George," whispered Mrs. Gallagher.

"Would they keep the records right here in the sanctuary?" asked Allyn. Of course, she knew the answer to this question already.

"No, Allie. We'll have to check in the parish offices here," answered her aunt.

"Uh, Mom, while you and Aunt George talk to the priests, would you mind if I had some time in here alone? It's really beautiful, and I just feel like sitting and praying a little in here."

Mrs. Gallagher agreed but asked her not to approach any strangers. St. Eunan's was a well-known tourist spot, and Mrs. Gallagher wanted Allyn to be cautious.

"Can I stay, too, Mom?" asked Mitchell.

"I don't think that's what your sister had in mind, Mitchell," replied Mrs. Gallagher.

"Well, yeah, I guess it'd be okay if Mitch stayed, too," said Allyn, glancing at Mitchell's anxious face. "If he can be quiet."

"I can be quiet! Watch me! I can be real quiet," answered Mitchell.

Mrs. Gallagher told Allyn and Mitchell that she didn't know how long it might take to search for the records. She told them not to leave the sanctuary and that she would be back in about fifteen minutes to check on them.

As soon as her mother and aunt had disappeared, Allyn whispered, "Mitch, quick! Follow me, do what I do, and don't say a word."

Allyn took off her shoes, and Mitchell did the same. Very quietly and carefully, she stayed close to the back wall and then moved behind the table with the information sheets on it. Fortunately, the young man didn't turn around. Standing diagonally, the table was in a corner, and there was just enough room for Allyn and Mitchell to crouch behind it without being seen.

It was 4:02 p.m., and Allyn was worried that she

had picked the wrong man. A few seconds later, however, there it was! A familiar voice! It was Fisher, the one who would recognize them, and Allyn found herself shivering. She glanced at Mitchell, and he had gone pale. *I've done it again,* she thought. *I've pulled my brother into something awful.*

Inching around the side of the table to hear better, Allyn tried to breathe as softly as she could.

"Maybe you'll use them again," said the young man. "In a year or two James might be back in Ireland or somewhere in the Isles."

"Don't count on it," replied Fisher.

Allyn couldn't hear anything for a few seconds, and she was afraid they were suspicious.

"Too dangerous to you, are they?" asked the young man.

"The Triad keeps itself clean," said Fisher.

"When — after the concert?"

"No, no. The jet," said Fisher. "An accident ... but a *thorough* accident."

Allyn's heart was pounding so fast she thought she was going to faint.

"We heard that James doesn't know anything," said the young Irishman. "Tony, Buck, Louis, Bill, Jack — that's it. No one else. They were afraid he'd blow the whole deal. So your organization, it must know James has been out of it. If the drop is smooth, he'll never know. The band's been kept blind about us. They're no threat to Caloran. So why — with ten times the men, ten times the money — has your end been so sloppy?"

"A mistake," answered Fisher in irritation. "New York — one of our men said that all five, the whole band, overheard the word *Triad*. A fatal mistake. That's all it takes for the trace back. My employers can't afford that."

"So you're sayin' James has got to be a casualty, too."

"Can't be avoided," answered Fisher coldly. "They'll all be on the jet. We're wasting time! Give me the details so I can get out of here. I hate religious places."

"Second payment in Loughshinny then, as we agreed," said the Irishman. "We have an informant in INTERPOL. They're watchin' Caloran, but they haven't a clue who's in the network. Caloran won't be anywhere near Dublin, as a diversion. If all goes well at the arena, you'll meet with Dirk — bald with a blonde moustache — at The Blue Bell Pub, at 10:00 p.m., two hours after the pick-up. Your associate, he'll be in Dublin then?"

"Yeah," answered Fisher. "He did the southern part of this deal."

"Remember — you've never seen or heard of any of us," warned the Irishman. "We have our own cleanin' system, Mr. Fisher."

She was going to sneeze! It was cold in the church, and Allyn was going to sneeze! She was going to sneeze and be tortured and killed by smugglers who didn't care she was only a kid!

Allyn smothered her nose with her hand, but no use! A sound! A big enough sound that the men turned to look! She grabbed her shoes, pushed Mitchell out the other side of the table, and made a mad dash for the door!

Allyn heard Fisher behind her: "I know those kids! Get 'em!"

She pushed Mitchell out the main door, and they had just seconds to hide. "This way!" she screamed, and headed for garden shrubbery near the parking area. Allyn and Mitchell had just crawled into a row of thick bushes when the men appeared and split up to check the grounds.

Allyn couldn't see Mitchell's face. It was buried in the bushes, but she imagined he was terrified. She had to save him! She had to think of something *fast*!

The Irishman disappeared behind the back of the cathedral, but Fisher was close — too close. Allyn prayed that Mitchell would be absolutely quiet. Any sound at all would be the end. Fisher was a killer; that much she knew.

Slowly, thoroughly, Fisher was checking the nearby bushes. Just a few steps away ... and then, "I'm late!" shouted the Irishman, as Fisher met him behind a huge statue, about thirty feet from Allyn and Mitchell.

"Mitch," she whispered. "I've got an idea. Do you have your little pocketknife?"

"Yeah," Mitchell said faintly.

"Follow me — *very* quietly, Mitchell."

Crouching behind the bushes, Allyn reached the first row of cars. There were just a few, and it was easy to spot the one she wanted. Mitchell was right behind her, and she stopped at the familiar blue rental car — Fisher's car.

"Give me your knife, Mitch," she whispered.

"No, Al. I can do it," he answered, with courage that surprised Allyn.

"Okay — right here. Puncture it."

Mitchell stuck the knife hard into the back left tire, and Allyn quickly motioned for him to follow her and to hide behind a car farther away from the men.

"Mitch, I know our car's locked. We gotta think of a way to get to that other building over there. That's where Mom is, unless she's back in the church already, looking for us."

Just then, Allyn caught a glimpse of the Irishman heading for the parking lot! They were in trouble! Allyn and Mitchell were in clear view of the exit to the street, and if they moved to hide in *front* of the car, Fisher would see them from the garden.

"Mitch, get your shoes on quick! Wait until the Irish guy backs up in his car. He's going to see us then, so run as fast as you can after me!"

The Irishman started his car, backed up, and headed for them on his way out of the parking lot. Allyn sprinted across the street, and Mitchell was close behind her! Then the Irishman's car started to follow them! Allyn made sure they stayed on the right side and went *up* the street, because the Irishman's car had to stay in the left lane.

"Stop!" he shouted from his window. "You kids better stop or you'll get hurt!"

Fisher had spotted them from the garden, and he wasn't far behind — on foot! Allyn grabbed Mitchell's arm and pulled him down a busy street, perpendicular to the cathedral. They dodged people on the sidewalk, and Allyn was so out of breath that she was sure they'd be caught and killed.

"A cop!" yelled Mitchell.

Allyn reacted instantly and pulled Mitchell in the direction of the uniform. "Sir — " She was panting too hard to say any more.

"Look, Al!" Mitchell was pointing to Fisher, who was now crossing to the other side of the street and pretending to ignore them.

"Look at what?" asked the garda.

"Oh — he's just nervous," explained Allyn. "Sir, we're lost. We need to find St. Eunan's. Our mother's there, and she's really going to be worried."

"You're not far," said the garda, smiling. "You just go straight up the street here. You'll see the steeple in front of you."

"Uh, Sir, if you don't mind — " Allyn was shaking, and she started to cry.

"Oh, no need for tears there," said the garda warmly. "I see you've been frightened. Follow me then." He put his hand on her shoulder and led them up the street.

The Irishman's car was nowhere in sight, and Allyn hoped he had gone. Fisher, though, had stopped in a shop doorway, and he was watching them as they walked up the street.

When the garda walked them into St. Eunan's, Mrs. Gallagher cried out and hugged them hard. Seconds later, however, she was upset. She was more than upset! She had been looking frantically for over fifteen minutes.

"They've had quite a scare, I think," the garda told her. "I'm sure they won't be wanderin' again."

The garda was thanked effusively by both Allyn's mother and Aunt Georgette, and then he left.

Allyn, swallowing yet *another* lie, told her mother that she and Mitchell had gotten lost while trying to find an outside entrance to the parish records building. Mrs. Gallagher was still too upset to care about these details; she paid little attention to Allyn's explanation and, instead, lectured them both about the dangers of wandering outside alone in an unfamiliar place.

In Allyn's heart, though, she was genuinely repentant. She was sick of lying — even for a worthy cause; and she was very sorry she had frightened her mother. As she and Mitchell climbed into the safety of their car, Allyn wanted to bury her spy notebook and forget everything they had heard and seen and done. A part of her felt like she was still being chased, and she hadn't recovered yet. At that moment, the only thing that mattered was to get out of Letterkenny and never see Fisher again!

Allyn and Mitchell leaned back, and just as they were beginning to relax, *there* was Fisher! Close! Close enough to see Allyn clearly through the glass! She watched him as he ran back toward St. Eunan's parking lot. Allyn guessed that he might have stayed to watch the garda — whether he would return to his post quickly or not. Fisher would know that the garda would take the time immediately to report something if he had been told about the conversation in St. Eunan's.

Allyn knew that Fisher would be furious when he returned to his car. Truly furious! She winked at Mitchell, and Mitchell managed a smile. They had done it! It was hard to believe that they were actually driving out of Letterkenny alive!

Mitchell seemed fine for about ten minutes, and then Allyn noticed that the old paleness was back.

"Aunt George, could you maybe stop?" asked Mitchell, holding his stomach. "I'm gonna be sick."

Aunt Georgette spotted a parking place in front of a restaurant and stopped quickly.

"Come on, sweetheart," said Mrs. Gallagher, taking Mitchell into the restaurant.

Aunt George began telling Allyn about the "lead" she had gotten from the parish records, but Allyn was so distracted she could hardly hear her. The horror of what Fisher had said to the Irishman was coming back. She needed to write everything down as soon as she could.

"He should be better now," said Mrs. Gallagher, as she and Mitchell got into the car again. "I think we all need a rest."

Mitchell was completely white, and Allyn felt responsible. She squeezed his hand, and then she got out her spy notebook to write what she could remember. Already, she had forgotten a lot of it. When she had listed the new notes, Allyn stared at Mitchell, who was leaning against his door and trying to sleep. He still looked bad, and she felt guilty. She had dragged him into something frightening, and she had encouraged him to puncture a tire — a *very* bad thing, even if it was for their safety.

After dinner at Lennon River House, their bed-and-breakfast in Rathmelton, Allyn and Mitchell passed up watching Irish television in the big common room and went straight upstairs. Mitchell had hardly eaten anything, and now he was quietly drawing. They talked a little, but Allyn felt like being quiet. She pulled her knees up to her chin and sat with her arms around her legs. That afternoon she had heard news that frightened her so much she couldn't think of anything else. Darryl James was innocent, and awful men were trying to kill him in his jet!

Allyn turned the pages of her notebook again. She hadn't written much about the talk:

— A jet accident to get rid of the band members and Darryl
— Darryl James is innocent!
— Fisher meets Dirk (bald, blonde moustache) at The Bluebell Pub in Loughshinny, at 10:00 p.m., 2 hours after the pick-up

Allyn had heard something about a contact at INTERPOL, but she couldn't remember any more details. She was glad she had remembered the meeting place and time in Loughshinny.

"He's innocent, Mitch. He hasn't done a thing," she told her brother, who had stayed behind the table and had missed hearing most of the contact meeting.

Mitchell looked up at her for a few seconds, but, oddly, he didn't say anything. A few minutes later, though, he asked, "What are we gonna do now, Al? Should we tell the cops, 'cause we know Darryl James didn't do anything bad."

"I wish I knew what to do, Mitchell," answered Allyn, trying to stir up enough energy to think. "The band arrives in two days, the concert's three days away, and in five days Darryl James flies back to New York. I know one thing, Mitch. We can't let him get in that jet again to fly back."

"Why don't we just go to the cops?" Mitchell suggested again. "I think they'll believe us, Al. And Mom and Aunt George can help us."

"I know, Mitch. But there's a problem. If we get the gardai involved now and they pick up the band at Swords — "

"Swords?" interrupted Mitchell.

"The airport near Dublin, remember? Even if they get the drugs there, the gardai might not catch any of the Irish contacts because *they* won't be at the airport." Allyn was feeling a little better. She needed her whole mind tonight. Sitting up straight, she explained the rest. "I think — and I'm not sure — but I think the pick-up is going to be in the dressing rooms at 8:00 p.m. on the night of the concert, Mitchell. I heard a name in Drumcliffe, and I didn't write it down because I couldn't exactly remember it. I knew it was a strange name, and when I heard the Irish guy say 'Dirk' today, something clicked. I'm pretty sure *that* was the name of the guy who's supposed to be in the dressing rooms."

Allyn handed her notebook to Mitchell. "Look — Dirk meets Fisher at 10:00 p.m., and that's supposed to be *two hours* after the pick-up," explained Allyn. "It's got to be at 8:00. But, Mitch, they can't be talking about the night they arrive in Ireland. It has to be another night."

"Why, Al? Seems like it'd be better to get rid of the stuff right away," reasoned Mitchell.

"The magazine said that Darryl James isn't supposed to arrive at the airport until 7:45 p.m. on the nineteenth. Do you see what I'm saying?"

"Not yet, Al."

"It takes a while to get through the airport, Mitch — longer than fifteen minutes, for sure, to get through the airport and to get to Loughshinny. And maybe Darryl James and the band aren't even staying in Loughshinny overnight. Maybe they won't go to the arena until the next day. If Dirk will be in the dressing rooms at 8:00 p.m., then I think it has to be the night of the concert, Mitchell. The concert begins at 7:30, and I bet they'll do it right afterward — at a time when no one would suspect a smuggling deal."

"Let's go tell the cops, Al. They could plant somebody at the concert."

Allyn looked at him and didn't answer immediately. Here she was — the big sister — and Mitchell had the only sensible idea.

"Mitchell, I think there's only one way to make sure the police don't arrest Darryl James."

"Why would they arrest him? You said he was innocent."

"Think about it, Mitchell. It's *his* band, it's *his* jet, and it's during *his* concert. The gardai would never buy the idea that he was totally innocent! And even if the band members would be decent enough to try to tell the gardai that, they probably wouldn't believe them, either. After all, they're drug smugglers! I'm sure Darryl James would be booked as an accomplice, Mitchell. I know they'd send him to jail. But I guess anything that would keep him off the jet would be good. We've got to keep him off that jet, Mitchell!"

"Is there any way we can show the police that he didn't do it, Al?"

"I don't know, Mitch. The only way they would really believe it is if they found out about the plan through Darryl James himself. *He's* got to be the one to tell them."

"But he doesn't even know about it! How can he tell 'em anything?"

"That's a good question." Allyn was quiet for a few seconds, and then she smiled at him. "I guess we'll have to tell him first, won't we? Yep — we'll just have to tell him first," she repeated in almost a whisper. "What I don't know yet ... is how."

Climax at the Concert

Allyn spent a restless night in Rathmelton, and the restless feeling got worse as the next two days passed. As they were driving through the southwest corner of Northern Ireland, Allyn's arm was full of half-moon nail marks — a sure sign of trouble. Inside, she was carrying a very heavy weight.

She was wondering who Fisher and Gundersen's Chinese bosses were and if they lived in the "big" China — the People's Republic of China. Maybe there was an American branch of the organization, but the bosses kept themselves anonymous by staying in China. Or maybe the Chinese bosses lived in New York and were from the "little" China — the Republic of China on the island of Taiwan. Allyn knew that it was much easier to leave Taiwan than it was to leave the People's Republic of China. The People's Republic didn't have a democracy, and people had to get special permission to travel into other countries. Allyn got the two Chinas mixed up a lot, so she remembered them by thinking that the big, mainland country had most of the people, and people was in its name.

Allyn had a friend in school who was from the Republic of China (Taiwan), and she really liked her. Allyn had gone to her house for dinner, and she had loved being around people whose customs were so different from her own.

Even though she knew a few things about both Chinas, Allyn had never heard the word *triad* before. Her guess was that it was another name for Fisher and Gundersen's bosses, and it was such a big secret that people were killed for even hearing about it. From what her aunt had told her about the word, Allyn wondered if the triad was a group of *three* Chinese bosses who ran a crime network and had some people working for them in New York and Ireland.

"Only half an hour from Loughshinny, Allie!" said Aunt George enthusiastically. "I bet you're excited about the concert!"

"Yeah. Oh, Aunt George, you have no idea how important it is for me to see Darryl James," answered Allyn, and she glanced at Mitchell and winked.

"I bet! Getting to see your favorite singer feels like a matter of life or death!" said Aunt George.

Mitchell looked at Allyn, and they both had to cover their mouths to keep from laughing.

Soon they were passing a "Loughshinny" sign, and Aunt George pointed out the carnival grounds. There was a huge open area and then the concert arena. Apart from these grounds, though, there was almost nothing else in Loughshinny! It was just a tiny village.

They looked at street signs to find the way to Eire Rest, Mrs. Shine's bed-and-breakfast place. *Eire* was an Irish word for "Ireland."

While they drove through the main part of the village, Allyn glanced to her right, and there it was! Right there was a tiny sign in front of a pub — *The Blue Bell Pub*! Allyn felt a kind of chill along her spine. It existed! Seeing The Blue Bell jarred her back to reality. She had very little time to come up with a plan.

It was four o'clock, and they were in time for Mrs. Shine's afternoon tea. Allyn had learned that *tea* in Ireland meant more than a boring bag in a cup. Tea meant luscious homemade pastries and cheese and fruits. Tea meant pleasure! Tea could mean hippo hips if she weren't careful!

After two of Mrs. Shine's scrumptious pastries, Allyn and Mitchell sat on the sea wall behind Eire Rest and brainstormed. "Mitchell," Allyn told him, "speak now or forever hold your peace."

Mitchell shook his head "no," as a huge purple bubble expanded from his mouth.

"There's only one way to do it, Mitch. Just before the concert begins, I'll give beautiful, wonderful Darryl James a note. And then I'll kiss him all over his face."

Mitchell rolled his eyes and licked the exploded bubble from his lips.

"You brought that extra-long mural paper, didn't you?" Allyn asked. "And you brought the markers?"

"Yeah. I'm doin' the first part of my art project on it. Then I'm s'posed to keep addin' things to it and — " Mitchell stopped and searched Allyn's face. "No! No, Al! You can't have it! You can't have all the rest of my paper! I need it! I want an 'A' in art! It's my best subject, and it's the only 'A' I'm gonna get! And I kept all the paper real clean, too, inside my leather folder."

"Mitchell, this is *very* important. I don't ask you for much. I have hardly ever, in my entire lifetime, asked you to do anything for me — for ME, Mitchell, your ONLY SISTER! You have no one else, Mitchell. Even Marley's gone now."

"Don't mention Marley! It was part your fault, anyway!"

Allyn had touched a delicate subject. "Okay, let's put that behind us," she said with an amiable smile. "The important thing is that you and me, kid, we're *partners*! We work well together. We're saving a life — A LIFE, Mitchell! In fact, if we can get these bums picked up, we'll be saving lots of lives. Just think of it, Mitch — think of what we'll prevent in Ireland."

Mitchell was moving around uncomfortably.

"Yes, Mitch, it's a heavy responsibility — the kind of thing the army does every day."

He was weakening.

"Of course, you're only nine years old, and I shouldn't expect you to understand things like army missions."

"I do understand, Al! I'm years ahead of where I should be!" he insisted.

"Well ... well, that's very interesting, Mitchell. So I suppose you'd be willing to assist me in *this* dangerous mission, too?"

"Yeah! I'm good at that stuff! You saw yesterday — I saved us! I saved us with the pocketknife!"

"Hmmm, that's very true, Mitchell. But *dedication* means a lot in the army. Being dedicated means giving up things we really like — things that are important to us. That long, long roll of paper, for instance."

Mitchell nodded soberly.

"To you, that paper is for a mural, an art project which *could* be done at home where Mom has more paper like that. But to Darryl James and hundreds of Irish kids, Mitchell, that paper is the difference between life and death."

Mitchell was pulling her sleeve to get up. Inside, he gave her the paper, and in half an hour Allyn was done with the message — a huge message, printed in block letters on the long paper. "You won't regret this, Mitch. You've done an important thing today," she told him.

"Soldiers are steel," Mitchell answered solemnly.

Aunt George had planned a fun time in Dublin. Although it took a long time to drive in and out of the city, Allyn had a great time. They had a fancy dinner and heard a good Irish singer. At night, Dublin reminded Allyn of a city like Washington, D.C. It seemed friendlier than big American cities, though.

When Allyn woke the next morning, she didn't want to get up. They hadn't gone to bed until after midnight, and she knew that today would be the longest, most important day of her entire life! During the morning and afternoon, everything passed by her like a blurry dream. Allyn couldn't concentrate on anything, and she even had trouble eating. All through the afternoon, in fact, she felt as though the lively sport of racquetball were happening in her stomach. She decided that life as a criminal investigator was not easy!

Finally, it was time to drive to the concert. All through the afternoon, cars had jammed the streets of little Loughshinny. There were newspaper people and people from Irish television and people arriving very early for the concert. Parking was not easy. Aunt George had to park far away from the grounds, and Allyn was glad she was wearing jeans and her running shoes.

Dublin at Night

Allyn had a note in her pocket, and Mitchell had his leather folder with him. When his mother had asked him if he *really* wanted to draw during the concert, Mitchell told her that he wanted to sketch Darryl James and then lizards for his back-up band.

When they walked inside the arena, the place was mobbed, and it was a relief to find their reserved seats were still empty and waiting for them. To Allyn, it was a wonderful feeling to be on the front row in such a huge crowd; the seats seemed to go back forever. She realized that her father must have paid a fortune for their tickets, and it made her wish he could be there with them. She shivered when she realized how important being on the front row had become. It would give her a last chance to save Darryl James from jail.

There was no curtain and no one was on stage yet. The roadies had done their job, though; the sound equipment and instruments were set up and waiting. There was no sign of the instrument cases.

The lights were very bright because the American T.V. crew was there, and there were four cameras: two about halfway back, on both sides of the arena; and two between the first row and the stage. The cameras in front of the stage were high, and the cameramen were practicing turning the cameras. Allyn figured that during the concert the cameras would probably shift between shots of the stage and shots of the audience.

There were two security gardai about one fourth of the way back, and Allyn could just barely see uniforms much farther back. As she looked at the gardai, she wondered how quickly they would react when they learned about the smugglers. With such a big crowd, it would be hard for the Irish police to move anywhere quickly. Allyn hoped there were gardai outside, too, near the backstage entrance.

She looked again at the note in her hand:

Dear Mr. James,
    Your band smuggled drugs into Ireland in their instrument cases.
    Irish dealers are going to pick up the drugs at 8:00 tonight in the dressing rooms. Please tell the gardai now and save yourself! And people are going to make your jet crash!

Mitchell was sitting on her left, and Allyn shielded the note from the stranger on her right. She was *very* nervous! She was going to do something that might humiliate her and save Darryl James's life at the same time! Her mother would think she was nuts; millions of Americans watching would think she was nuts; Jeremy Sherwin would turn on his television at just the wrong moment and decide she had the brains of a rutabaga.

It was 7:30. Allyn's heart was beating faster and faster. The lights flashed on and off; people started cheering; and band members walked on stage and got their instruments ready. Then — then — yes! Darryl James! The real Darryl James! Lifesize! Allyn was sure he was the most beautiful human being that ever walked the earth.

For ten minutes, Allyn tried to put the note out of her mind. She listened to the first song with tears in her eyes, and the applause and cheering were so loud that Allyn told Mitchell they'd need an ear transplant after the concert. Her aunt was used to wildness, but Allyn wondered how her mother would survive it.

Then, when the second song was just beginning, Allyn decided she had better act now! She clutched the note and raced up to the stage — raced and climbed directly up, without the side steps. She handed the note to Darryl James just before a crewman was pulling her off the stage. Humiliation! There was wild laughter from the crowd. But she had done it! She had given away her dignity for Darryl James!

Mrs. Gallagher was three seats away, on the other side of Mitchell and Aunt George. Allyn glanced at her as the crewman led Allyn back to her seat. Her mother was absolutely livid.

From the stage, Darryl James thanked "the girl who gave me the note" but asked the audience to please consider *sending* him their fan mail. Everyone laughed again — everyone but Allyn and Mrs. Gallagher.

After changing seats with Mitchell, Mrs. Gallagher searched Allyn's face and whispered, "Why? Why would you do such a thing?"

Allyn, amazingly, was numb to everything. As her mother was waiting for an answer, Allyn watched Darryl James slip the note into his pocket without reading it. She looked at her mother and didn't know what to say. Leaning to her ear so she could hear her, Allyn said, "Mom, I know it's hard to believe, but I had a really good reason. There's too much to explain now, but I promise I'll tell you all of it later. I really need for you to trust me right now. I've never needed you to trust me so bad in my entire life!"

Her mother looked confused. "I don't think I'm going to like this," she told her.

It was 7:51, and Allyn panicked. "Mom, I need to do one more thing — something that people do at concerts all the time."

Before her mother could answer, Allyn got Mitchell's attention. He was sitting on the other side of Aunt George now, and he took the sign out of his folder. He crouched in front of his chair and stretched to give Allyn the other end of the sign. They unravelled it in front of the first row, but so low to the ground that it didn't block anyone's view.

Allyn had moved a few feet away from her seat, and her mother was whispering, "Allie! Allie, *please!*"

"It's okay, Mom!" she told her anxiously. "It just says 'We love you, Darryl' on it!" Allyn swore to herself that this would be the very last lie she would tell for the rest of her life.

The sign, of course, had a very different message:

YOUR BAND SMUGGLED IN DRUGS! PICK-UP AT 8:00 TONIGHT IN DRESSING ROOMS!

What happened next is concert history! When the T.V. cameraman on the left turned his camera away from the stage and focused low to get a good shot of the sign, one of the band members leapt off the stage to talk to the cameraman. Whatever he said made the cameraman turn the camera back toward the stage. While this was happening, though, Allyn was watching Darryl James. He kept singing, but he was looking at the band member.

As soon as the song was over, Darryl James did something unbelievable. He stopped to take out the note and read it! Allyn was so nervous that she could hardly breathe.

"I'm sorry for this delay," announced Darryl James, "but someone has brought a problem to my attention and — "

Instantly, without waiting for more, two band members ran for the wings of the stage and disappeared!

"Stop them!" yelled Darryl James in a commanding voice. "Security! Gardai! Look for drugs in the dressing rooms!"

The other band members put down their instruments and began talking with each other. They turned their backs to the people and to Darryl James, who was trying to calm down the audience. "Please — please stay in your seats," he pleaded. "I'm so sorry about this. If you're willing to stay, you'll get a concert — I promise you."

There were cheers, and then people got quiet when two gardai led the other band members off the stage. Allyn wanted to know exactly what was going on, but she knew her mother wouldn't let her go backstage. She guessed that the two other band members must have been caught and then told the gardai that they *all* were involved. It was a relief that the gardai hadn't taken Darryl James off the stage! Still, Allyn kept thinking about the Irish smuggling network and hoped the gardai had found someone in the dressing rooms.

Darryl James looked shaken and sad, and Allyn felt so sorry for him. She thought it was incredible that he would stay and sing while his friends were being marched away. Allyn decided that people who were really *professional* entertainers put their feelings aside in order to do their jobs.

For forty-five minutes, Darryl James played his guitar and sang. When Allyn turned around to look at the faces of the crowd, people seemed both confused and supportive. She and Mitchell, though, were the only two who understood what had really happened.

When Darryl James took the note out of his pocket, Allyn's mother and aunt had asked Mitchell and Allyn to turn the sign around so they could read it. Allyn and Mitchell complied, and Aunt George stared, open-mouthed, at the paper. She was so stunned she couldn't speak.

Mrs. Gallagher's face went from shock to disapproval, and then her eyes filled with tears. She got out a tissue, and a few seconds later whispered to Allyn, "I don't know what's been going on, and I'm very *very* upset with you. I can't believe you didn't tell me! We'll talk about all these things, Allie, and I've got a *lot* to say!" Her mother was quiet for a few minutes, and then she added, "I'm not sure any of this is actually happening!" She hesitated, wiped her eyes again, and smiled. "But, Allie, I do need to tell you, to say something to let you know ... just, just how proud I am." At that point, Mrs. Gallagher hugged Allyn and cried again.

Unbelievably, instead of sending people home at nine o'clock, Darryl James announced that he would do the second half of his concert, too. He said there would be a fifteen-minute break and that then he would continue the concert if the gardai had no objections.

The Blue Bell Pub! The thought struck Allyn

like a shotgun. "Mom! I need to talk to the security chief *right now*! It's really important!"

Surprisingly, Mrs. Gallagher didn't question this and immediately got up to lead Allyn to the garda in charge.

"Sir," explained Allyn, "I'm the one who told Darryl James about the drugs. But there's another criminal, too! Could you maybe write this down?"

The garda nodded without smiling, and he got out a small notepad.

"There's going to be an American — with short black hair, a black moustache, handsome, and probably in his late twenties — at The Blue Bell Pub at ten o'clock tonight, right here in Loughshinny. He was supposed to get money for this drug deal. His name is Fisher, and he's really nasty. Can you send somebody there right away?"

The garda promised her he would. Calmly, he asked them for their names, where they were currently staying in Ireland, and the date of their return flight. Then he wanted Allyn and her mother to follow him outside for some more questioning. Allyn knew this would be a long ordeal, and she pleaded with him to let her hear the rest of the concert. He finally agreed, but said that she needed to report to security immediately afterward.

Allyn enjoyed seeing how surprised her mother was at how much information she and Mitchell had collected in Ireland. The break was extended an extra ten minutes, but it went quickly. As the second half of the concert began, Mrs. Gallagher whispered, "Your father will never believe this. I'm here, and I don't believe it!"

Allyn actually relaxed a little during this second half of the concert. Other than giving the Irish police her spy notebook, she had done everything she could. As she watched Darryl James play and sing, Allyn felt that the danger and the tension and the planning that had filled her whole vacation in Ireland had all been worth it.

There was incredible cheering now and a standing ovation when Darryl James finished his last song and bowed. Everyone was clapping and clapping for an encore, and suddenly a stranger was standing in front of Allyn and giving her a folded piece of paper. With so much noise in the background, Allyn couldn't ask him anything. The stranger didn't try to speak, either. He smiled, handed her the paper, walked to the outside aisle, and disappeared.

It was stationery — Darryl James' stationery! The paper had his personal letterhead at the top, and the message was that Darryl James would call her at Eire Rest at 11:00 the next morning. Allyn's name wasn't on it, but she was amazed that Darryl James must have taken the time during his break to write it and to ask the security gardai where she and her family were staying. She wanted to kiss the paper! Instead, though, she showed it to her mother, who looked surprised and pleased. Then Allyn folded it again with tender care and put it in her pocket.

Although he didn't do an encore song, Darryl James did return to the stage to make a statement about had happened. He apologized and also took responsibility for the actions of his band, but he assured people that he had known nothing about his band's involvement with drug-trafficking.

After Darryl James bowed again and left, people clapped for a long time. Finally, when Allyn turned to put on her coat, a young girl approached her.

"Allyn Gallagher?"

Allyn looked at the stranger, and it took several seconds to connect this girl with her photograph. "Fiona?"

The girl nodded.

Allyn grabbed both of Fiona's arms and looked closely at the girl's face. "It's really you! It's really you — in person!"

Fiona laughed. "You can thank me mum. She got tickets for Claire and me, but far, far in the back there. When I saw you on stage, Allyn, I knew it had to be you! I knew you were givin' all your spy stuff to Darryl James!"

"And, Fiona, it worked! I told you it would be okay if I waited!" exclaimed Allyn, still looking at Fiona as though she were a dream.

Mrs. Gallagher and Aunt George and Mitchell

had crowded around Fiona to meet her. Allyn intro-
duced them, and Mrs. Gallagher asked Fiona if she
wanted to stay the night with them and to go back
the following day.

"Thank you, Mrs. Gallagher," answered Fiona,
"but we promised our parents we'd stay in Rush
tonight with my aunt. She hasn't seen us in a long
time. Me mum would be upset if we skipped that!
But, wait, you haven't even met my sister Claire.
Claire! Claire!" Fiona waved to her older sister, who
was several rows back and talking to some other
teenagers.

Claire seemed shy but pleased to meet
Americans. "I admire what you did," she told Allyn.

"Thanks, but I hope they caught all the guys. I
told the chief garda and — " Allyn suddenly remembered something important. "Mom! The chief! We're
supposed to talk to the security chief!"

Mrs. Gallagher was convinced that meeting
with the gardai so late would not be wise, because
all of them were exhausted. She said she would
request a long appointment with the Irish police
tomorrow. In the meantime, Allyn could stay and
talk with Fiona and Claire for a few more minutes.

When Mrs. Gallagher returned, she had a garda
with her; he had been ordered to stay near them
throughout the night and on their way to gardai
headquarters the following day. In fact, he said that
he might be near them for protection until they left

for America. If Fisher was still on the loose, they were in danger. Allyn was sure that he was clever enough to find them, no matter which B-and-B they chose.

On the way back to Eire Rest, Mrs. Gallagher told them that they would probably have to leave a day later — on October 22 — and that the Irish police had offered them free first-class seats for the trip. The garda's car was directly behind them, and it did make Allyn feel protected. The garda would be taking a room for the night in Eire Rest, too.

Going to sleep was impossible! Allyn and Mitchell were tired, but they were both too bouncy and excited to sleep. Although she said nothing to Mitchell about it, Allyn was also feeling something strange — an uneasy, restless feeling. There were smugglers who could recognize her. She had done something dangerous on national television. Allyn turned on the light, and she and Mitchell played cards and talked.

When Mrs. Gallagher knocked on the door, Allyn thought her mother would tell them to turn off the light immediately. To Allyn's surprise, both her mother and aunt came in, and all four of them sat talking for over an hour. Allyn related every detail she could remember, and her mother's face went through every possible emotion. At the end, both Aunt George and Mrs. Gallagher were hugging and kissing Allyn and Mitchell and telling them how sorry they were that the Drumcliffe and Letterkenny experiences had been so awful and frightening.

Of course, Allyn knew that there were still some loose ends, so it wasn't *quite* all over. Tomorrow she would tell the gardai about Darryl James's jet and would ask whether they had caught Dirk and Fisher.

Something wonderful would happen tomorrow, too. Tomorrow, she — Allyn Lane Gallagher — would get a phone call from gorgeous, fabulous Darryl James himself.

The Trace and the Answers

Mitchell was tugging at the sleeve of Allyn's pajamas and announcing that morning had come. In fact, half the morning had gone by the time Allyn opened her eyes.

When she and Mitchell finally went downstairs to breakfast, Aunt George and Mrs. Gallagher were already sipping their coffee and reading a Dublin paper. There was no mention of last night's events yet, but Allyn guessed the papers would be full of the story by tomorrow.

It was hard for Allyn to enjoy breakfast when she was so excited about Darryl James calling her. She ate a little, and then her aunt noticed something in the parking area. The garda was in his car and dutifully watching Eire Rest, but Aunt

Georgette said that another police car was parking.

A few seconds later, Aunt George exclaimed, "I don't believe it! It *is* him!"

Allyn turned around to look, and there he was! Darryl James! With a garda, Darryl James was walking into Eire Rest!

"Oh, there you two are!" said Darryl James warmly as he walked into the dining area. "Last night I asked the security garda if he knew where my young rescuers were staying. I wanted to thank you and to find out exactly how you discovered all these things."

"Please — please, sit down!" said Mrs. Shine, insisting that Darryl James and the garda have tea and bread.

He was so handsome. His blonde hair waved at just the right places, and Allyn decided that his eyes were liquid turquoise, like some wonderful tropical lagoon.

At first, Allyn could barely push words out of her mouth. It was such a funny feeling to chat with the person whose picture she had kissed passionately in the privacy of her own room! When she had calmed down a little, Allyn got out the stationery and thanked him for the note.

Darryl James stared at the letterhead and at the message and frowned. "I didn't write this, Allyn."

Mrs. Gallagher put her hand over her mouth and looked petrified.

Allyn felt a chill go up her back. "Mr. James, why would somebody want to talk to me?"

The garda interrupted, "We're goin' to find that out. Now don't you worry," he said to Mrs. Gallagher in a comforting voice. "You'll all be safe in Ireland."

Within half an hour, the garda was joined by men from a special investigation unit, and they were preparing to trace Allyn's eleven o'clock call. As the gardai and Darryl James and Mrs. Shine and Allyn's family sat tensely in the kitchen and waited for the phone to ring, Allyn was told that she should stay on the line as long as she could.

The phone rang.

Allyn's hand was shaking when she picked up the receiver. On the other end was an Irishman's voice, telling Allyn that he was Darryl James' secretary in Ireland and that Mr. James was busy with some unexpected guests. The Irishman told Allyn that Darryl James was very interested to hear how she had learned about the drug-smuggling plan.

"Sir, I really don't know much about it," she told him. "I overheard someone talking about the band smuggling drugs into Ireland and about the pick-up at the concert at eight o'clock."

The gardai were nodding that she was doing a good job. They had warned Allyn to tell no one that she could identify *faces*.

"I didn't see who was talking." Allyn tried to steady her voice. "And, well — that's really all I heard. I like Darryl James, so I wanted to tell him about it somehow, and that's when I decided to write a note and to do the sign."

"And, tell me, where exactly did you overhear this?" asked the stranger.

The gardai were close to getting the trace.

"Uh, I'm trying to remember the name of the place," said Allyn slowly, stalling for time. "It was one of those little towns — a village-type place. He had an angry voice."

In a chair a few feet away, Mrs. Gallagher was ashen white and so nervous that Aunt George was standing behind her and almost holding her shoulders up.

Allyn swallowed hard and hoped they would get the trace any second now. "Is there anything else you wanted to know?" she asked.

"Just one thing — do you think you would be able to recognize the angry voice if you heard it again? Mr. James is anxious to find out who was working with the band. And the gardai might want you to stay in Ireland until they have some suspects."

With her right hand, Allyn's nails were making those familiar half-moon marks all over her left arm. "Oh, no — I need to get back to school in America. I really couldn't help the police, because I'm not so good with voices. And I didn't hear any names, either. I guess angry people all sound the same to me." She knew this was a dumb line, but at least the gardai were nodding that they had gotten the trace.

The Irishman made up some story about Mr. James sending his "best wishes," and then he hung up.

She had done it! Everyone applauded, and Allyn collapsed in one of the chairs. She felt as though she had just run a marathon.

Darryl James got up and kissed her on the cheek. Allyn smiled at him and decided she would never wash her face again! She would preserve this tender, meaningful moment for the rest of her life!

What followed were three very interesting days — days that established Allyn as a genuine criminal investigator. Allyn and Mitchell were key witnesses, so the flight home had to be postponed until the evening of October 24.

During two of the three days, Allyn had been taken to a different kind of gardai headquarters and had gone over the details in her spy notebook with a man who had an American accent. Her guess was that this man was from INTERPOL, although he never mentioned for whom he was working. He was, however, *very* interested in the idea that there might be an informer working inside INTERPOL.

Allyn asked him about the word *triad*, and his answer was close to what Allyn had already guessed. The Triad was a Chinese criminal organization, like the Mafia. It was based in the United

States, but it operated all over the world. The symbol for the organization was a triangle, with each side standing for one of the three basic ideas of Chinese life: Earth, Man, and Heaven.

"Do all Chinese people know about the Triad?" she asked.

The agent laughed. "No — of course not. Just because you're an American doesn't mean that you know about American criminals, does it? And your Irish heritage shouldn't make you feel responsible or guilty for this Irish drug network. Be sure you learn this — *never* assume things about people, Allyn — not because of family connections or race or nationality. Everyone is different, and everyone deserves to be judged for who they are, as individuals."

Allyn liked him a lot. In fact, she thought he was as smart as her father. The agent asked her to call him "Mr. Kohlman," but she guessed that he wasn't giving his real name.

There was still something about the whole plan that made no sense to Allyn. She asked Mr. Kohlman why Fisher and Gundersen would risk meeting with these contacts all over Ireland; she thought it would have been smarter and less risky to mail any money or information.

Mr. Kohlman disagreed. He said that the Triad liked having a sense of complete control in any operation and that they didn't trust the mail system in any country for confidentiality. They were hesitant about using either telephones or computers, too. Much of their important business was done through direct meetings. Also, they had probably instructed Gundersen to get to know the area contacts in Ireland, possibly because they might want to bypass Caloran someday as a "middleman" and employ the contacts directly in the Triad. Then Fisher was sent both to help Gundersen meet these contacts and also to make sure Gundersen's method of arranging these meetings was effective and secretive. Mr. Kohlman added that, as Allyn had written in her notes, Gundersen knew that Caloran might be an INTERPOL "subject of surveillance" (Mr. Kohlman's term for *suspect*), so meeting with Caloran directly was avoided.

Allyn asked about the ferry runs and if Caloran's network had people working for it in Great Britain and France. In response, Mr. Kohlman said that there were probably contacts working at the ferry ports in Wales, England, and France. He doubted, though, that there were a large number of people in Caloran's employ *outside* of Ireland.

Mr. Kohlman also explained that there were probably other Triad members temporarily in Ireland. Others had bribed officials at Swords Airport and in Loughshinny, for example. The Triad typically protected itself by giving many different people limited information and very specialized jobs.

O'Connell Bridge, Dublin

Allyn appreciated how patient Mr. Kohlman was with her questions; it was important to Allyn to understand what she and Mitchell had uncovered. After her first meeting with Mr. Kohlman, Allyn could piece together most of the smuggling plan. The Triad had arranged for the band to take the drugs into Ireland, and the Triad would pay them well for the smuggling. The Triad, however, remained anonymous when they made the deal with the band. When the band overheard the name of the organization, they became a threat to the Triad and were supposed to be killed in a jet accident on their return to the United States.

In Ireland, the Triad was selling the drugs to Caloran, whose contacts would keep half the drugs in Ireland to sell there and send half on ferries out of Ireland. Gundersen and Fisher would collect the Triad's payment.

What really amazed Allyn was that the Triad bosses, the people who made the most money from the drugs, weren't anywhere near Ireland. They never had to see the drug-users: the teenagers who actually took the drugs and whose lives were ruined because of them. She thought that if people would just stop buying the drugs and using them, then these big criminal organizations would stop making money and would collapse. At least she had done something to stop *this* drug deal.

During Allyn's second meeting with Mr.

Kohlman, he prepared her to do something difficult.
The gardai had caught Fisher just as he was leaving
The Blue Bell Pub at about 10:45 on the night of the
concert. Dirk, of course, hadn't shown up with the
money, because Allyn had stopped "the drop" at the
concert. Allyn wished the gardai had let her know a
few days ago that they had gotten Fisher! They were
able to keep him in jail because "Fisher" was using
a fake name and passport, and the gardai were
checking into his background.

Mr. Kohlman met Allyn at the drug-investiga-
tion unit headquarters, and he took her into a
strange, glassed-in room. She felt a little faint when
she saw both Fisher and Gundersen standing with
several other men on a platform, and it was a relief
when the gardai told her that she couldn't be seen
from outside the room. She identified both Fisher
and Gundersen as the Triad's men involved in the
drug deal.

Gundersen's capture had been a surprise. When
the gardai had traced Allyn's mysterious phone conversation to a Dublin lounge, they found the Irish
stranger who had given her the note and called her.
There, too, was Gundersen! They had taken
Gundersen in for questioning, because he fit the
description Allyn had given the gardai. As expected,
Gundersen's passport, too, had phony information.

The Irish stranger in the lounge had been with
Dirk at the concert. During the concert break, this

stranger and possibly others had acted fast. They wanted to know just how much damage Allyn's information could do, so they came up with the plan of calling her. They stole Darryl James's personal stationery from backstage, wrote the note, and then must have asked a bribed garda for the name of Allyn's B-and-B. She and her mother had just given that information to the security chief.

Unfortunately, the gardai hadn't been fast enough to catch Dirk, who had left the arena without picking up the drugs. Allyn wondered, however, just how many of the gardai had been bribed by the Triad not to get Dirk. The good news, though, was that this Irishman from the lounge promised to give information about Caloran's network in exchange for a lighter sentence.

The final detail was that Allyn wanted Darryl James's jet to be checked for problems or explosives and to be guarded round-the-clock until he left Ireland. Allyn was surprised that the Irish police and Mr. Kohlman were treating her with adult respect. It was a great feeling!

On the morning of October 23, Allyn and Mitchell and their banner sign posed for a photograph for *The Dublin Times*. Also, that afternoon, Allyn got great news. The gardai's security force had found evidence of tampering in the jet's engine, and they were correcting it. They assured her that Darryl James would have a safe trip back.

In gratitude for all that Allyn and Mitchell had done, Darryl James took the four of them out to dinner in Dublin the night before they left Ireland. For Sally, Darryl James wrote an "affectionate note," and Allyn was sure Sally would tape it as close to her heart as possible. For Allyn, there was a promise from Darryl James: he *would* be in touch, by mail or by phone.

On the evening of October 24, as they arrived at Swords Airport, Allyn realized that for two weeks she had forgotten all about North Carolina and her little problems there. So much had happened in Ireland that it made all the other struggles in her life seem very small.

Allyn's father would be so shocked by her story that she would have to tell him the details over and over again! Allyn was glad she had a souvenir to give him. She and Mitchell were taking back four copies of a Dublin newspaper. On the front page were Allyn and Mitchell, smiling broadly — smiling and holding their brilliant "smuggler sign" for the Irish world.

For more information
about traveling in Ireland, contact:

THE IRISH TOURIST BOARD
345 PARK AVENUE
NEW YORK, NY 10154
TEL: (212) 418-0800
(800) 223-6470

Several generations after McGinleys left County Donegal for good, Carol McGinley returned to explore the culture and spectacular Irish landscape for herself. Her travels throughout Ireland supplied the inspiration and ideas for *Allyn's Embarrassing & Mysterious Irish Adventures*.

After teaching English and tutoring for nine years, Ms. McGinley began writing full-time. She is currently completing both a nonfiction project and a comic work about a rural newspaper columnist. She lives in Apex, North Carolina.

Order ***Allyn's Embarrassing & Mysterious Irish Adventures*** from AGA Publishing or from your local bookstore.

ORDERING INFORMATION

Price: $10.20 (For U.S. residents — includes price plus $2.25 shipping & handling)

$10.68 (NC residents — includes 6% sales tax plus shipping & handling)

$11.45 (Canadian shipments — includes ground postage)

To order with Amex, Visa or Mastercard, call:
(919) 387-4568
Or **fax** your order to: (919) 303-7111

Please include the following with all orders:
— Name and address, include city, state, zip
— Quantity requested and total price (with S&H; tax)
— Telephone number (with area code)
— For credit card orders, include complete card number, expiration date, and name as listed on card
— For check or money order payments, include with order

Send all mail orders to:

 **Publishing, P.O. Box 513, Apex NC 27502**

Allow four weeks for delivery in the continental U.S. Call for shipping information to other countries.

Quantity discounts available.